the fairy godfather

THE CHANCELLOR FAIRY TALES, BOOK 3

MELANIE KARSAK

THE FAIRY GODFATHER
The Chancellor Fairy Tales, Book 3
Love Potion Books, 2016
Copyright © 2016, 2018 Love Potion Books
Previously published as *The Bee Charmer* under Melanie Karsak's nom
de plume Poppy Lawless. All rights reserved. No part of this book may
be used or reproduced without permission from the author. This is a
work of fiction. All characters and events portrayed are fictional. Any
resemblances to the living or the dead are purely coincidental.
Lines in Chapter 1 are adapted from William Shakespeare's *A
Midsummer Night's Dream.*
Editing by Becky Stephens Editing
Proofreading by Rare Bird Editing

"All our dreams can come true, if we have the courage to pursue them."
Walt Disney

rayne

The sound of the honey bees buzzing all around me was sweeter than any Vivaldi concerto I'd ever heard. I sat lotus style in the apple orchard, inhaling the sweet scent of the apple blossoms. My eyes closed, I could feel the white petals falling on me as a soft wind sent them spiraling. The warm spring sunlight shone down on my face. It must have been almost noon. The rays of sun felt warm on my skin. I listened to the bees hum as they danced from flower to flower. Perfection. I inhaled deeply, and with each exhale, set my enchantments on the wind:

Bring a love for Alice.
Now is the time.
Bring a love for Alice.
One that's finer than wine.

Wine? Not a very good enchantment, and not a very good rhyme. No wonder Alice was no closer to meeting the man of her dreams than she'd been the day I met her three years ago when I'd gotten my assignment.

Wine...of course it would be wine. Ever since I'd set eyes on Viola Hunter, the dark-haired wine heiress who just happened to be the sister of my best friend, I'd been distracted. I imagined her skipping nymph-like through the apple orchard under the spring sun. Imagining, however, was as far as I'd ever taken anything. Viola Hunter, whose family's vineyard sided my small country farmhouse, had already friend-zoned me. There was little use pining over a woman who just wasn't into me. After all, Alice was supposed to be my focus. I needed to shake Viola from my thoughts. Poor Alice. I was doing my best, but she still wasn't where she was supposed to be. I needed to try harder.

I shut out all thoughts of Viola Hunter and set my mind on Alice once more. I tuned into the sounds of nature: the humming of the bees, the rustling of the new leaves, and the feel of the warm sunlight on my skin. This time, I lifted the willow wand sitting in my lap and gave it a wave as I intoned:

Over hill, over dale,
Through brush, through brier,
Over park, over pale,

Through flood, through fire
Bring Alice her love!

This time when I said the enchantment, I could feel the magic. A little sound, like the chiming of a hundred small bells, told me that the spell had worked. I could almost see my words glimmering like gold on the wind, twisting and turning upward toward the sky in search of the one who would bring Alice's heart joy.

I opened my eyes and looked down at the wand. For a moment, I wished I could just give it a wave and have everything I wanted. But that wasn't how this worked. Whatever I wanted, I was going to have to work for it. Good thing I didn't need much. But the moment I thought it, Viola came to mind once more.

My phone, lying in the grass beside me, buzzed. I picked it up to see I'd received a text from Alice. So soon? When I opened the message, however, I was perplexed.

Crisis, she'd written.

What's wrong? I answered back.

Dumped again. Bring chocolate.

I sighed heavily. When Alice started dating Tom, Chancellor's local sheriff, I knew it wasn't meant to be. He wasn't a bad guy, but they were completely wrong for one another. And I also knew that uniting Alice with her true love meant that Tom would have to go away. But that fast? Wow, maybe I was getting better at this than I thought. Or maybe, it was just time.

On my way into town now. I replied.

There was no answer. It was the midday lunch rush at Alice's bagel shop. No doubt that would keep her busy, her mind occupied. I frowned. Also, it was the worst time of day to get dumped.

"Time to get to work," I told the bees. They stopped their tasks then and swarmed, making a passing spiral around me, from my feet to my head. I could sense their questions, their excitement.

"Help me?" I asked. "Help me find the one for Alice?"

With an excited buzz, they flew off happily. I had no doubt they'd do everything they could.

"Thank you," I called behind them then headed out of the orchard.

My old pickup sat waiting near the barn. Shielding my eyes with my hand, I gazed across the horizon at the row after row of vines owned by Viola's family's business, Blushing Grape Vineyards. I could just make out the roof of the Hunter family's elaborate mansion sitting along the shore of Lake Erie. So close, but so far away. I sighed and looked out at the lake; the waves were dark blue that morning. The wind blowing off the lake was still cold, even though it was April, but I could feel the earth coming back to life. Spring had come again.

I picked up the cases of honey I'd packed up earlier that day and set them in the back of my truck. Sliding into the driver's seat, I glanced once more at the Hunter family mansion. Where was Viola today? Working at the estate? Was she busy at the family restaurant downtown? Or was she over at the college where she'd started taking classes once more? The image of her laughing and running through the orchard played again through my mind.

Alice. I needed to focus on Alice.

I lifted my phone again. Still no reply from Alice.

"Sorry, Alice. I'll try to do better. Looks like you're stuck with the worst fairy godfather ever."

CHAPTER 2
viola

"For next class, be sure to finish the equations on pages seventy-six and seventy-seven and prepare for your exam on chapter thirty-two," Professor Wallace said, scribbling on the board.

I quickly scrawled the assignment down in my notes while wondering when in the world I was going to get everything done. I needed to give up sleep. That was all there was do it.

I cast a glance at Meredith who was sitting beside me.

She shook her head. "And in a few weeks, finals. Are we having fun yet?"

"Of course," I replied with an eye roll. But the truth was, as hard as it was to work and study, I was having fun. In fact, I was the happiest I'd been in a long time. My first three years of college had been amazing. My grades had been great, I'd made lots of friends, and I was starting to get a good grasp on where I was going in life. And then, Mom had died and my world had fallen apart. Dad needed my help at the family business so I'd set my goals aside to help out. But then everything just snowballed. Dad took Mom's death hard. It changed him. And little by little, I found myself running more aspects of Blushing Grape Vineyards than I'd ever intended. I didn't mind my family's business. In fact, I actually loved enology. I loved to create new vintages, new flavors. It wasn't a far leap from my true passion, which was perfumery. But that passion had been put on hold. I didn't want to play the role of wine heiress any more than my brother Horatio had wanted to play a wine baron. But, thank goodness, those darker days were over now. My dad was back to his old self, taking over aspects of the company once more. My brother had a new job, a new girlfriend, and a new life. And me, I'd reenrolled in college and was just coming to the end of my first semester back. In a year, I'd have my degree and be able to start chasing my dream.

"See ya," Meredith called then headed out.

I waved to her then finished packing up my things.

"Viola?" Professor Wallace called.

Hoisting my bag over my shoulder, I approached the

podium. Professor Wallace was a slip of a man, perhaps my father's age, with thinning white hair. He was touted as one of the hardest chemistry professors on campus, and while the work was tough, I knew I was learning a lot. I wanted to understand the science of what I was doing, and a degree in chemistry was just what I needed. While other students in the class were, no doubt, studying to become doctors or scientists, my motivations were much different, and Professor Wallace was one of the few who knew about my passion.

"Professor?" I asked politely.

"Thank you very much for preparing the programs for the symposium. I know our department administrative assistant appreciated your help."

"Anything, professor. The symposium is going to be a wonderful event," I replied. In was, in fact, honored when Professor Wallace asked me to help out in preparation for the chemistry symposium that would be held that week. If working at my father's company had taught me anything, I knew that networking was a key to success. Wherever people were doing things I was interested in, that's where I needed to be. And this week, that was the research symposium.

"Oh yes, oh yes. We have some really excellent minds coming in. The sister city group is sending a delegation from Japan. I think your brother is working on the sister city event?"

I nodded. In addition to the research symposium, this was a busy week in Chancellor. Every spring, Chancellor celebrated its relationship with our sister city, Narashino, Japan. And this year, my brother was organizing the festivities. "Yes, Horatio is overseeing that project. He's organizing the Cherry Blossom Ball."

"Very good," Professor Wallace said with a nod. "Now, Miss Hunter, I was hoping I might ask your help once more?" he said as he slipped his yellowing lecture notes into his worn, brown satchel.

"Of course, professor."

"As you know, we've got a number of scholars and professionals coming in from all around the world to deliver papers. There is one gentleman, however, I think might share your interests. Luc Beaumont is a scholar from the Provence area. He is a chemist, of course, but his main business is—"

"Luc Beaumont? The perfumer? From the Beaumont brand?" I asked, unable to control my excitement.

The professor smiled. "You've already heard of the Beaumont family. I had assumed so."

I smiled. "I...I studied all the French perfumers. I was hoping, one day, to study abroad in France at a perfumery."

"Yes, I remember reading that in your reflection essay. Seemed serendipitous, I thought. Now, would you be willing to meet Luc Beaumont? He'll arrive in Chancellor tomorrow. The college has lodged him at Lavender Fields Bed and Breakfast. In your guise as both a student and a Chancellor notable, would you be willing to show him around? The college is rather keen on impressing him. The Beaumont family would certainly prove excellent benefactors to our college. And it was President White who suggested I ask your help."

Caught. Definitely no way to say no now, not that I would anyway. "Of course, professor. Tell President White I'm happy to help."

Professor Wallace nodded. "Good, good. Here is his information," he said, handing a paper to me. "I'll let him know to expect you."

"Of course." This was a golden opportunity. Monsieur Beaumont was a preeminent perfumer. His family had been in the business of crafting fragrances for hundreds of years. And he had several apprenticeship programs.

"Very well, very well. Thank you, Viola. Oh, and well done on your research paper. Your analysis of bee pheromones was very well researched."

"Thank you," I said, smiling. "I'll check in with

Monsieur Beaumont tomorrow. Thank you, and President White, for the opportunity."

He nodded then turned back to packing up his bag.

Clutching the paper, I walked out of the classroom. Well, my Hunter name had put me under the spotlight once more, but I could hardly be angry. More than anything, I wanted to study perfumery in France. Meeting Monsieur Beaumont and charming the pants off him was just the chance I needed—though it wouldn't have to go as far as actually *pants off*. Luc Beaumont was probably my father's age. What I was really going to need was the hospitality of a wine heiress mixed with the charm of a Disney princess.

I pulled out my phone, turning the volume back on since I'd set it on silent for the duration of the class. When I did, however, I saw I had a text from Alice.

Come to the deli when you have a chance?

Just out of class. You okay?

No. Can you come?

Yep. On it like a bonnet, I replied back then hurried out of the chemistry building and across the campus green. It was a beautiful spring day. The wind blowing off Lake Erie was crisp and fresh. The air smelled sweet. I could smell daffodils and hyacinths in the air. Lovely. I stuffed the paper Professor Wallace had given me into my bag and walked toward town, which sat at the bottom of the hill along the lakeshore. From this viewpoint, I could see all of Chancellor, including Falling Waters, the restaurant my family owned. I had enough time to stop by Alice's deli before I needed to get ready for work and the evening dinner rush. I sighed. I loved Chancellor, but I was ready to do what I wanted to do. No doubt I would miss it here when I went to Provence for an internship at Beaumont perfumery.

rayne

The engine rods in my old truck knocked a few times after I switched off the ignition. I hopped out and grabbed the boxes I'd stored in the back. Heaving up the box of goods, I walked into The Curiosity Curio. The little shop sat along a refurbished alleyway in which one could also find a bookstore, a smoke shop, an imported foods store, and a small French restaurant. I pushed open the door to the small antique stop and was instantly met with the strong scents of old books, polished wood, and other interesting, aged aromas.

Tess, the shop owner, looked up from the jewelry cabinet where she'd been working. "Hi, Rayne," she said in her quiet voice.

I noticed she had four pieces of old jewelry set out on the cabinet. Like many of the items in the shop, something struck me as off about those four pieces. They had an odd shadow to them, much like the antique store owner. Being a faerie living in the human world afforded me a sense of sight most humans didn't share. I was able to notice all sorts of otherworldly touches, most of which escaped human notice. And in Chancellor, well, if regular people knew just how different the little college town actually was, they'd be surprised. All those witch and fairy tales that made up the town's folklore were more than just legend. But who was I to tell them what they couldn't see? And besides, there were more things that went bump in the night in Chancellor than even I understood. In some cases, I could sense something was different, but I never knew just what. Such was the case with Tess and her little antique shop.

"Just restocking my booth," I said, glancing down at the jars of honey, candles, and bottles of body lotions. The Curiosity Curio was, in fact, a co-op of curiosities. While most of the booths in the shop offered antiques, there was also a section for local goods like jams, fishing flies, and the local beekeeper's wares.

Tess smiled, the small gesture making her petite face, framed by a mop of dark hair, light up. "Almost out of the honey-carrot body butter."

"Brought some. Back in a few," I said then went toward the back. I set out my goods, restocking the shelves. My honeys were selling well, and tourist season in Chancellor would kick into full swing soon. No sooner did the students leave than the antiquers and other connoisseurs of quaintness would start coming into town. But at the moment, the upcoming Cherry Blossom Ball would draw many visitors to Chancellor. The ball, which was the highlight of the sister city event, would bring dozens of well-to-do families to Chancellor, all of whom loved to purchase curious things.

After I'd unloaded my wares, I stopped by Pat's chocolate booth and picked up a box of sea-salt caramel dark chocolates shaped like mermaids then walked to the front where Tess was waiting.

The girl smiled then set a box on the counter. "Finally got your box lot from the auction packaged up. The hive tools you wanted are on the top. There were some other interesting items in there as well. Go through them when you have a chance," she said, sliding a cardboard box toward me.

The week previous I'd spotted some antique honey making tools at an auction but had to buy a whole box of knickknacks to get them. "Thanks, Tess," I said, then set the box on the floor. "Grabbed some chocolates," I said, setting them on the counter. "Do you want cash or—"

"I can take it out of your commissions, if you like."

I nodded. "Thanks."

"Of course," she said then motioned to the box once more. "Don't forget to look through the box. Never know what you'll find."

This time, I raised an eyebrow at her. Tess was different. There was an unusual aura about her, and she seemed almost immune to the faerie twinkle in my eyes. Today, something more was going on, but I wasn't sure what.

She cocked a funny smile at me. "See you later," she said, then turned from the counter and went back to sorting vintage pins.

I grinned. Whatever her mystery was, I wasn't going to get it out of her today. "See ya," I replied, lifting the box, then headed back outside. I exited the little alley and went back to Main Street. It was past the lunch hour now and downtown was quieting. I stopped by the truck, leaving the box of knickknacks—mindful that I should look through them when I had a chance—then walked to Alice's deli, Whole Lot 'o Bagels.

The bell over the door rang when I entered. All at once, I was treated to the heavenly scents of freshly baked bagels and french onion soup. I could even catch the perfume of the daffodils with which Alice had decorated the small café tables. But more than that, I also heard the sad and lonely sounds of breakup music wafting through the deli's speakers. The remaining diners didn't seem to notice, but the woman behind the counter was working furiously to clean every last corner of her deli, a tell-tale sign all was not well.

"Sea-salt dark chocolate caramels," I said, setting the box on the counter as I pulled out a stool.

"Finally," Alice said, tossing her cleaning rag into the sink. She stopped to wash her hands then came around from behind the counter, pulling off her green apron. She set it aside as she redid her ponytail, pulling her dark hair back into messy bun. Her freckled face had lost its cheery glow, her dark blue eyes looking sad and haunted. She sighed then shook her head. "Dumped by text, can you believe that?"

That was pretty low, even for Tom. From the moment I met him, I knew Tom was not for Alice. But Alice always had a way of sneaking off and finding exactly the wrong guy when I wasn't looking. Her last fairy godmother had worked with the elders to bring her a good match a few years earlier, an archeology professor visiting Chancellor College, but the professor's fate had got in the way. He'd made an unexpected archeological find on an island in Lake Erie which turned his attention away from a potential life mate to his passion. That flop had displeased the elders, and not long after, I took over the job looking after Alice. Alice, however, was proving more difficult to help than any of my other assignments. And my personal distractions—mainly in the form of

Viola Hunter—weren't helping much. But these days, all the signs seemed to point to something big on the horizon. The bees saw omens everywhere, and this morning's powerful enchantment was even more proof.

I gave Alice a hug, squeezing her tight. "He wasn't right for you anyway," I said, then let her go.

"Yeah, I know," she said. "I just couldn't get into his Monday night football scene. I mean, I don't mind football, but the appetizers at those parties. Ugh," Alice said with a mock-shiver.

Typical Alice, trying to make light of her own misery. I opened the box of chocolates and slid it toward her. "The right guy is coming. I can feel it. I think it's time, don't you? I'm going to find you someone great."

"Don't you mean we? We are going to find her someone great?" a female voice asked coming up from behind us.

I turned to find Viola standing there. A million smart replies wanted to fly out of my mouth, but all I could do was smile stupidly at her. How amazingly perfect she looked in her dark jeans, black sweater, black boots, and a designer bag turned school book bag hanging off her shoulder. Her long, chocolate-colored hair glimmered under the slim rays of sunlight that shimmered into the room. Her sky-blue eyes, the same color as Horatio's— her brother and my best friend—searched my face.

"No smart comeback?" she asked.

"Sorry, I was just struck dumb by your beauty."

"Oh my god, shut up," she said, punching me playfully on the shoulder, but her eyes flicked toward me for a moment thereafter, shooting me a warm glance that set my heart on fire. "Sorry, Alice," she said then, turning to her friend as she settled onto a stool next to me.

"Yeah, what can you do? My prince will show up one day."

"I hope he has a brother," Viola said.

The bell rang once more as the door opened. I looked toward the back of the deli where I spotted Amanda, a regular patron at Alice's, and a group of her friends come in.

Amanda smiled at me. "Hi, Rayne," she called in a soft voice then she and her friends sat down.

I waved then turned back to Alice and Viola. While Alice might have had her problems finding a man, the faerie glamour under my skin had no problem attracting women. Sure, I was handsome enough, but it was the faerie twinkle in my eyes that caught most women's attention...save Tess'. When I was feeling playful, it was fun to let the twinkle do its work. I'd found myself the attention of many beautiful girls along the way. When on assignment, however, we weren't supposed to be distracted by dalliances...human or faerie. And for the most part, I'd done well keeping myself to myself. I'd been a fairy godfather for almost ten years and had a good track record. Patching two hearts together had always come easy. And when the job was done, I always moved on to the next assignment. Chancellor, however, was the first place that had ever felt like home. I loved my little farm. I loved Chancellor, where the unusual seemed to live on every corner. I, myself, being unusual by human standards, fit right in. But there was nothing unusual about my kind. The faerie had been living among humans since the time of legend. We just didn't "out" ourselves. While there weren't any rules preventing us from sharing our lives with humans, most faeries found it easier to stick with our own kind, as my parents had and theirs before them. Our kind had their own work to do. Looking after Alice just happened to be my job. After my work was done, I was going to ask to stay in Chancellor. It was time for me to do something different. It shouldn't be too much of an issue. After all, I wasn't the only faerie in Chancellor.

Interrupting my thoughts, Alice said, in a low, jesting voice, "Wish I had Rayne's twinkle."

"Seriously, tone it down, Rudolph," Viola said, mock-shielding her eyes. "You're going to end up with half the women in Chancellor in love with you."

"They aren't already?" Alice replied.

"It only takes one," I said. "The right one." I looked

at Viola who, I was pleased to see, had cast a passing glance at me. Not for the first time did I wonder how she felt about me.

"Isn't that the truth," Alice said with a smile, then rose. "Well, better see what the girls want to eat."

Viola also stood. "I need to get home and change before I head over to Falling Waters. I just wanted to stop in and make sure you're okay," she said then turned to me. "You're going to be here for a while? Don't want Alice to be alone."

"Of course. Alice offered to make me lunch."

"I did?"

I winked at her, causing her to roll her eyes at me.

Viola then turned and hugged Alice once more. "Don't worry. The right guy will come along. Who knows, the ball is coming up. Never know who you'll meet. You're still coming, right?"

"Well, I was going to come with Tom. But, yeah, what the hell. I bought a dress already. How about you? You have a date?"

Viola shook her head. "Too busy to worry about something like that."

"You rope Rayne in yet?"

Viola turned to me. "Horatio invite you?"

"The Cherry Blossom Ball?"

"That's the one. You're coming, right?"

I grinned. "Am I?"

"Yes. Who else is going to escort me? And thanks for asking," she said with a wink. "Oh! Do you have a suit? Jeans and flannel won't work."

"I'm not a heathen. And yes, I'd be happy to take you."

Viola smiled, and this time her eyes met mine. "Thanks, Rayne," she said, lightly setting her hand on my shoulder.

"My pleasure, Miss Hunter."

Viola smiled. "Okay," she said, turning to Alice. "I need to go, but call me if you need me, okay?"

Alice nodded. "Gonna whip up a big batch of hazelnut chocolate cream cheese and some cinnamon bagels and carb away the sorrows. Thanks for stopping by, hun."

Viola smiled at me once more, and with a wave, walked back out.

Alice slipped her apron back on. She was fussing with the ties, not making eye contact with me, when she said, "Well, that was interesting."

"What was interesting?"

Alice looked up at me and raised an eyebrow. "You didn't notice anything interesting?"

"Interesting isn't the word I would have chosen."

Alice shook her head. "At least someone's making

progress," she muttered under her breath. "Decide what you want to eat. I'll be back in a minute," she said then went off to meet Amanda and her friends.

I looked out the window. Viola was already gone, but I imagined her walking up the street, her chocolate-colored hair glimmering in the spring sunlight. Had the woman I really wanted just asked me on a date? But was it a real date or a friend date? I wasn't sure. But for the moment, I let myself soak in the possibility that Viola Hunter might just share my feelings...and that idea set my world on fire.

viola

I parked my Mercedes in the driveway of our house, which sat among the vines near the lakeshore. A strong wind blew off the dark blue waters. My anxiety about my upcoming chemistry exam, along with meeting Monsieur Beaumont, work that night, and just about everything else, had my mind spinning. I needed to get to the restaurant. I had become the defacto manager of my father's new enterprise, Falling Waters, an upscale restaurant located in downtown Chancellor. This was both a good thing and a bad thing. Thankfully, I'd managed to hold Blushing Grape Vineyards and Falling Waters together until my dad could patch up the pieces of himself. While he was back at the helm, running the family company once more, I still found myself locked in. It was only on my dad's urging over the Christmas holiday that I went back to school. I was, after all, almost done with my degree in chemistry, and my dad was always partial to my idea that Blushing Grape should branch off and dabble in perfumes. Finally, I was getting somewhere. But it wasn't easy. School all morning. Work all night. Studying into the late night hours. I had to laugh when Alice asked if I had a date for the ball. Date? I barely had time for a shower.

I sighed as I glanced across the horizon. Vines surrounded our house on every side. Their sweet new leaves uncurled like tiny green fingers. The familiar cycle of the vines seemed to be almost part of me, having grown up around them all my life. And while I loved the grapes, my true love was flowers.

I turned and followed a path to the sprawling gardens behind the mansion. At the back of the house was a large patio area that overlooked the manicured grounds. The daffodils, tulips, and hyacinth were finally in bloom. The garden was alive with vibrant yellow, varying shades of pink, firehouse red, and deep, royal purple. I walked past the beds of spring flowers, stopping to pick just one tiny blossom off a hyacinth plant. What a sweet smell. Most hyacinth perfumes smelled too heavy. The scents of spring were for younger girls. Maybe if I mixed something citrus with the aroma, lightening the scent up with something tart and fresh, I could create something new, something surprising.

My cellphone buzzed, interrupting my thoughts.

I pulled it out to see that my alarm was going off. No time to daydream. I needed to get ready for work.

I gently glided my hand along the flowers, feeling their silky petals. Before I turned and went inside, I cast a glance west where I could just make out the roof of Rayne's barn. I smiled when I thought of him at the ball. He was going to look pretty hot in a tux. The more I thought about him and me going out for the night, the more I liked it. Who knew what could happen? A dance. A kiss. More? Ugh! Why did my thoughts of Rayne always go that direction? I mean, we were nothing more than friends, and I was about as far from his type as a girl could possibly be. With his good looks and that damned twinkle, he could date anyone he wanted.

But he didn't.

Why didn't he?

My alarm buzzed again.

"Okay, okay," I said, turning it off.

I turned and climbed the stairs to the back patio then entered the house. My mother's old grand piano was in the sitting room. With its amazing view of the gardens, I loved the space so much. I remembered Mom playing

Tip-toe Through the Tulips every spring in an attempt to make me and Horatio laugh. It always worked.

"Is that you, Miss Hunter?" a female voice called.

"Hi, Dorothea," I called to our housekeeper. "Just stopping in to get ready for work."

"Want any coffee? Need anything pressed?" she asked from somewhere in the house.

"No. Thank you."

"All right. You just shout if you change your mind."

I smiled. Dorothea had been part of our household for as long as I could remember. She and mom had been very close, and when mom passed, Dorothea had taken to looking after the three of us with new zeal.

I headed upstairs to my room on the third floor. Slipping off my school clothes, I grabbed one of what seemed like a hundred black cocktail dresses hanging in my closet. Hurriedly brushing my hair while I juggled my phone, I called Blushing Grape's administrative assistant.

"Hey, Judy," I said when she picked up, shimmying into the dress at the same time.

"Good afternoon, Miss Hunter. What can I do for you?"

"There is a gentleman by the name of Luc Beaumont arriving at Sweet Water airport tomorrow morning. I'll send you the flight details. Please call President White's office and let him know we'll send a driver to pick up

Monsieur Beaumont. Send the limo. He'll be staying at Lavender Fields Bed and Breakfast. Can you make sure he has a Blushing Grape executive gift basket waiting for him? Call Genevieve, the owner, and make sure he has the best room. Text me when you've got it all arranged?"

"Sure. Need anything else, Viola?"

"Not yet, but the day is still young."

Judy laughed. "Is it? It's almost four."

Dammit. I was going to be late. "Oh! Tell dad to sign the invoices I left on his desk. Let's make sure the vendors are paid on time."

"No problem."

"Thanks, Judy. Have a great night."

"You too, Viola."

Snapping a picture of Professor Wallace's notes, I zipped the information off to Judy then sat down at my vanity to quickly apply some eyeliner and lipstick. I shouldn't have sat. Tiredness swept over me. I'd been up late the night before studying for my comparative religions test. I thought I'd done okay. At least, I knew a whole lot more about the Sumerians than I had a week before.

I pulled my hair it into a tight knot at the base of my neck, smoothed out my black dress, and checked my makeup. Not bad. If anyone bothered to look, I might catch someone's eye. But even as the thought struck me, I imagined Rayne's bemused expression every time he saw me dressed like this. He always told me I looked beautiful, but half the time I thought he was joking. That damned twinkle, however, had a lot more to say, but I wasn't sure what. I could never quite tell if he was teasing me or not. Annoying.

Slipping on one of my favorite pair of Yoko Noir heels, I grabbed my bag and went back downstairs. I shook my head. Rayne. Why in the world did I care anyway what that hippie, and my brother's best friend, thought about how I looked? We were just friends, right? But even as I asked myself the question, a little voice inside me whispered the same thing it always did.

Yes. But what if?

CHAPTER 5

rayne

When I got home later that afternoon, I was surprised to find a VW van in my driveway, the owner sitting on my front porch.

I parked my truck, grabbing the empty wooden crates from the back, then climbed the steps of the porch to my old farm house.

"Hi, Cassidy," I said apprehensively. Cassidy, the other faerie who lived in Chancellor, had stripped off her sneakers and was rocking back and forth on the porch swing while blowing an enormous bubble. She'd pulled her long red hair into a pony tail.

"Great view. How'd you get these digs?"

I shrugged. "Luck."

"Leprechaun help you?"

I shook my head. "I don't deal with them. Sneaky buggers."

"Yeah. There's that. So, we're invited for dinner."

Uh-oh. "Really?" I asked, trying to shake off my obvious apprehension.

"Yep," she said, slipping her shoes back on.

"Do I need to change?"

She shook her head. "No, just the usual fare. Nothing fancy."

"Then I guess we'd better go?"

Cassidy shrugged. "Want me to drive?"

Hardly. Last time she drove, we almost died five or six times, but I wasn't about to remind her. "That's okay. I've got a full tank."

I set the wooden crates down by the front door then headed back down the stairs.

"Someone call you?" I asked Cassidy.

"Text."

I pulled out my phone. Nothing. Sometimes faerie etiquette puzzled me. After all this time with humans, couldn't we adopt a few of their better traits? I slid back into the truck and started the engine, Cassidy popping into the seat beside me.

"What's all this?" she asked then, picking through the box I'd picked up at the antique shop.

"Mostly knickknacks. I spotted some tools I wanted at an auction, but I had to buy the box to get them."

"Cute," she said, lifting some sort of figurine that looked like a cross between a troll and Santa.

"It's all yours."

She laughed. "Thanks," she said as she continued digging.

"I didn't even look. Anything useful in there?"

"Hum. Let's see. An old pot, some painted Easter eggs, chopsticks, some weird kind of vase, and this," she said, lifting a metal contraption. "What the hell is this?"

"An apple peeler, I think."

"Shoe box," she said, opening the lid to look. "Too small for me. Pretty though. Oh, here we go," she said, pulling out a little Hawaiian hula girl which she suction-cupped to my dashboard. "Perfect."

I laughed. Guiding the truck down the back roads, the hula girl dancing in tune with the potholes, I finally reached Route 5 which trailed alongside Lake Erie.

"So which one of us is in trouble?" Cassidy asked.

"Not sure. The bees say I'm getting close, but I'm still not there yet. How about you?"

"Um, yeah, she got into college but still no prom date."

"So...both of us?" I asked with a laugh, which Cassidy joined.

"Yeah, probably. I'm just going to focus on the onion rings. The diner has great onion rings."

I grinned. She was right. At least there was that.

WE PULLED INTO FAIRWAY DINER ABOUT HALF an hour later. The little restaurant, which sat along the lakeshore, was a landmark go-to place for college students to study...and sober up. The neon sign above the teal and chrome building buzzed as Cassidy and I passed underneath.

"Two?" the hostess asked. "We got a booth in the back."

Cassidy shook her head and glanced around. "No. We're with some people."

The hostess sized us up. "There?" she asked, pointing to the couple sitting near the back of the diner.

Great. Not only were they faerie elders, but it was Ziggy and Skyla, the elders who kept watch over the entire faerie community in the northeast. Cleary, one of us was in for a scolding.

"Crap," Cassidy whispered under her breath.

"Yep," I agreed. "That's them," I told the hostess who was smiling at me.

"Thought so. So, are you from around here or just passing through?" she asked me as she led us back to the table.

Distracted, I hadn't been paying attention to the glamour I was casting. In the presence of other faeries, my twinkly glow was buzzing so loudly that a few other women in the room looked up as I passed.

"Oh, no. My girlfriend and I are just here on vacation," I replied.

The hostess frowned.

Cassidy laughed.

"That's too bad," the woman said, clearly dejected, as she set our menus at the edge of the table. "Here you go. Waitress will be over in a minute." As the hostess walked away, I saw her frown sharply and shake her head, clearly chiding herself for the sudden flirtatious behavior that had swept over her.

Ziggy smiled at us as we slid into across the teal-colored vinyl seat, the upholstery groaning and crackling. The gold and silver flecked Formica table must have been freshly wiped down; it held the scent of bleach and dirty dish water.

"Rayne and Cassidy," Ziggy exclaimed happily. "We haven't ordered yet. Pick something. Dinner is on us."

I eyed the faerie elder. He looked, as always, like he'd just stepped out of the sixties. His long silver hair fell in loose locks all around his shoulders. The swirling designs of his multi-colored tie-dyed shirt accented the silver of his hair. He wore rings on every finger and strings of beads around his neck.

"Starving," Cassidy said. "They still have those onion rings?"

"I was going to get those too," Ziggy said then turned to Skyla. "What about you, Peaseblossom?"

"Salad," she said flatly then set down her menu.

Ziggy frowned. "Just salad? Who knows when we'll be back this way again? It's not like we get many problems from Chancellor."

"Okay, okay, salad and poutine."

"What's poutine?" Cassidy asked.

"Fries topped with gravy and cheese. It's a Canadian thing."

"Oh! I want that. I still need to get over to the falls. You two get over there much?" Cassidy replied. She was making small talk, but I noticed the tremor of worry under her nonchalant tone. Why, exactly, were we here again?

"From time to time. Rayne, you're quiet. Hungry, my boy?" Ziggy asked.

"I can eat. Alice filled me up at lunch, but I always have room for diner food."

"I took Twyla and her friends down to the bagel shop last week. They complained that I took them for carbs, but they ate all the same and have been raving about it since," Cassidy said, referring to her assignment, a teenaged girl name Twyla.

I smiled weakly then glanced at Skyla who was looking closely at me. Though she appeared to be around sixty in human years, her hair was a youthful sunflower yellow color. Her yellow curls tumbled over her shoulders. She was wearing a sundress with a sweater over it. Like Ziggy, she wore lots of jewelry. All faeries seemed to love shiny baubles. I couldn't help but notice, however, that she was wearing her infamous mirror amulet. While it looked like a simple piece of adornment, it was anything but. All faeries had their ways of keeping up with their work. The bees and I had our own routine, but everyone knew that Skyla could see quite a lot in that little mirror. I suddenly felt nervous. What had she seen?

Skyla opened her mouth to say something to me, but then the waitress arrived so she left the words unspoken.

"Ready to order?"

I waited patiently while Ziggy ordered for himself and Skyla, and Cassidy ordered just about every fried item on the menu.

"Sweet tea and fried pickles, please?" I said, not looking directly at the woman. This time, I was trying to make a conscious effort not to get her attention.

"Oh! Fried pickles. I missed that," Cassidy said. "An order of those for me too."

The waitress chuckled. "Sure thing, though I don't know where you're going to put it all."

"My boyfriend will help," she said, nudging me playfully in the ribs.

The woman laughed, shook her head, and walked off.

"Sorry about that, earlier, I mean," I told Cassidy.

She winked at me. "No problem."

"So," Ziggy began with a smile. "I bet you're both wondering why you're here."

I inclined my head and waited.

Cassidy, who was sitting lotus style on the booth seat, fiddled nervously with the laces of her sneakers.

"We've been keeping an eye on your progress...both of you," Skyla said, her voice sounding a little annoyed. "And the lack thereof. Cassidy, a prom date might seem like a small thing, but I have seen that it will have ripple effects on Twyla's life. You need to get a move on."

Cassidy nodded. "I totally agree. It's just the boys around her are just that...boys. I don't want her to spend all night trying to pry someone's hands off her butt. I can't seem to find—"

"I've seen someone...near the studio. In another wing in the same business complex. There's someone there," Skyla said, referring to the dance and yoga studio where Cassidy worked.

"The new fencing school, I'd bet. I'll start there. Thanks, Skyla."

She nodded.

"Rayne, we've seen your bees. Busy, busy, busy," Ziggy said.

I nodded. "I cast a strong enchantment this morning, and the bees think they are on to something. Someone is coming. I know it. I'm getting there."

Ziggy smiled. "We like Alice. Someone has been with that girl since she was just a mite. Hard nut to crack. She resists her fate at every turn. Stay on her."

"And don't get distracted," Skyla said, lifting her little mirror.

"Well, at least not until the work is done," Ziggy said, setting his hand on his wife's arm. "Right?"

The gesture seemed to soften her a bit. Skyla looked at me, smiling sympathetically. "I have seen your struggle," she said, looking from the small mirror to me once more. "All things have their season. Just see your work through. Remember your job. Your duty comes before any personal interests."

"And when you've got Alice all settled, we can see what to do with you next," Ziggy added.

"I hoped to stay in Chancellor."

Ziggy smiled. "You wouldn't be the first to stay there. Wasn't there a faerie who got mixed up with the Chancellor coven back in the sixties?"

Skyla nodded. "What a mess."

"Oh, that witch got him, but I don't think he minded much."

"Speaking of," Skyla said then, looking at me once more. "That friend of yours, Miss Dayton, is very observant. Be careful what you eat around her. She's got mischief in her mind. She's got a good heart, and the best intentions, just bad timing."

I grinned. Skyla was referring to Julie Dayton, the town's new baker, and Horatio Hunter's girlfriend. Her new shop, and especially her baked goods, were taking Chancellor by storm. What most of Chancellor's residents didn't know, however, was that her baking always had an extra special—even magical—ingredient. And I had already sensed that Julie had me in her sights. "You're right about that," I told Skyla. "Duly noted."

The faerie woman softened. "We know your work is challenging. Our assignments, however, need us. Some people come by their fates naturally, some need extra help. The young ladies in your care need you. If they didn't, you'd never be assigned to them in the first place. Do your best."

"Like I said," Ziggy added, turning back to his wife. "We rarely have issues in Chancellor. They'll sort it out. Right, kids?"

Cassidy relaxed. "Of course."

I nodded.

"Here we go," the waitress said, returning once more with a heaping tray, most of which she set down in front of Cassidy.

Skyla smiled. "I didn't think yoga teachers were supposed to eat so much fried food," she told Cassidy.

Cassidy grinned as she lifted an onion ring large enough to wear as a bracelet. "What? I eat when I'm stressed."

"Not a good way to cope," Skyla said. "Macrobiotic will clear out the stress faster."

"Or brownies," Ziggy added with a wink that made Cassidy laugh.

I smiled and sipped my drink. No distractions. They were right. Until I got Alice where she needed to be, I had to set Viola out of my mind.

Easier said than done.

CHAPTER 6

viola

"Night, Miss Hunter," John, one of the dishwashers, called as he left for the evening. "All finished in the back. Billy will take care of the last load."

From my position perched at the end of the bar, I waved to him. "Goodnight. Thanks for keeping us rolling at rush hour. Great job."

John smiled abashedly. "Thanks," he said then headed out.

I glanced at my phone. An hour left until closing. For a week night, Falling Waters had been busy. It was spring. Were the tourists on the move already?

I took one final bite of my lobster ravioli in brown butter sauce, scooping up the last langoustine on my plate. Perfection. One great thing about living near a college with a culinary arts programs was that we were never at a loss for amazing chefs. The dish had looked as pretty as it had tasted. Artfully arranged green and white asparagus, hand-made ravioli, sweet langoustines with lemon garlic butter, and a vibrant purple orchid, I wished I'd snapped a picture to post online, but I'd been too hungry. It had almost looked too pretty to eat. Almost.

"Sure you don't want a drink?" Rick, the bartender, asked me, and not for the first time.

I glanced up at him. With his wavy black hair, brown eyes, and a chiseled jawline that made Tatem Channing look like Jack Black, I'd be stupid if I missed the obvious signals he'd been sending me for the last month. But there were two problems. First, he was an employee. And second, he wasn't...what I wanted right now.

I shifted on the stool and slid my chemistry book in front of me once more. "I'm already so bleary-eyed that I can barely read. How about some coffee instead?"

"You're going to work yourself to death. Don't you ever take a night off?"

I smiled but cringed inside. It was coming. I knew it. "I'll take time off when the semester is over."

Rick nodded. "Then maybe when the semester is over, you'll come down to the marina and check out my boat?"

If I said yes, he'd think I was interested. If I said no, he wasn't going to let me study. I smiled. "Yeah, let's see how things go. I might take summer classes." Dodge. Avoid. I'd come up with another excuse later.

Rick smiled optimistically. "Okay, well, hope you can stop by. Let me put some coffee on for you."

I nodded appreciatively then turned back to my book. I swore I'd read the same page five times but still had no idea what it said.

"No, the bar is fine. We just want dessert," I heard a familiar voice say from behind me. Rayne?

I turned around to see Rayne enter with a red-headed girl I recognized but didn't know.

"Evening," Rayne said playfully. He helped his guest slide onto one the bar stools then slipped onto the seat next to me. "What's the subject tonight, my illustrious mad scientist?"

"Chemistry," I said, giving him an inquisitive look. What was he doing here and who was that girl?

"A subject you seem well-versed in."

"Oh really?" I replied with a laugh, shaking my head. "Ugh. This class is making potions with Professor Snape look like kindergarten."

Rayne grinned. "How about introductions?" he said, leaning back, "Cassidy, this is my friend, Viola. Viola, this is Cassidy. Cassidy is a family friend."

Cassidy, I noticed, chuckled.

"You have a family?" I asked Rayne with mock confusion. Truth be told, I knew nothing about where Rayne had come from. I always imagined his family lived on a commune or owned an organic salad dressing company or something. I had never actually met anyone from Rayne's world before. And now, his acquaintance was very....pretty.

"Hi," I said to Cassidy, reaching out to shake her hand. "You look familiar. Do you live here in Chancellor?"

She nodded. "I teach at the studio over by the high school."

I studied her. Her eyes, much like Rayne's, had a sort of odd sparkle. Was I right or was it just the dim restaurant lighting? She was very attractive. She had long, straight red hair, a smattering of freckles on her nose, and a lithe dancer's body. Yes, definitely pretty. And pretty familiar with my friend, from what I could see, as she settled in close alongside him. Her familiar nearness to Rayne set my nerves on edge. *Easy, Viola.*

"What can I get for you?" Rick asked them.

"Dessert!" Cassidy said excitedly. "I'm dying for something sweet. Rayne said you have the best desserts."

"And coffee?" Rayne asked.

Rick nodded. "Desserts. Tonight the chef has four dishes. We have a brandied cherry clafouti, which is brandied cherries inside a French custard, plantain mock-scallops with drizzled Belgian dark chocolate, a traditional crème brulee kicked up with lemon zest and lavender, and vegan cashew cheesecake with warmed brown sugar peaches served over the top."

"You're buying, right?" Cassidy asked Rayne, setting her hand playfully on his arm.

The muscles in my stomach tightened as an annoyed and jealous feeling sweeping over me.

Rayne shrugged. "Apparently."

"I'll try them all," Cassidy told Rick.

Rick smiled at Cassidy. Apparently I wasn't the only one who noticed her sparkle. "So, can I make you a drink?" he asked.

She shook her head. "Just coffee for me too."

"You're in luck. I've got a fresh pot brewing," Rick said then winked at me. With that he headed back into the kitchen to give the order.

I frowned and looked down at my book. Who in the hell was this girl? And why were both Rayne and Rick suddenly looking at her and not...well, not me. *Enough, Viola. Don't act like a spoiled brat. Not five minutes ago you were trying to think of a way to shake Rick. And Rayne is your friend. Don't be that kind of bitch.*

"Test?" Rayne asked, looking over my shoulder.

I nodded. "Day after tomorrow."

"So...Viola Hunter. I've heard so much about you," Cassidy said then.

Rayne passed Cassidy a glance but said nothing.

"Have you?" I asked, then looked at Rayne. "Do tell. What have you heard? I'd love to hear what Rayne has to say about me."

"Well, you are definitely as pretty as he said."

A massive butterfly spiraled through my stomach. "So, you think I'm pretty?" I asked Rayne playfully.

"A goddess," he replied with a wink.

"This is a great restaurant," Cassidy said then. "The water wheel outside is perfect. Just look at this place. Your family...the Blushing Grape people, right?"

I nodded. In most cases, being a Hunter was either a really good thing or a really bad thing. In the case of Cassidy, however, I heard no emotion at all in the statement. That alone warmed me toward her.

"I love your dessert wines," she said wistfully.

I smiled, a proud feeling swelling in my chest. I'd had a hand in developing most of the flavors for those wines. "Thank you. So, you teach?"

She nodded. "Some dance, I teach the little ones tap, ballet, and run mommy and me classes. Mostly I teach yoga though. At night I teach the older girls. I have a great class this year. Some real talents."

"How long have you been in Chancellor?"

"Oh, a bit. I just float with the wind. I started working at the studio last summer, helped with the choreography for their summer show. They put on *The Little Mermaid*."

I nodded. "I saw that show."

"You did? That's so cool. Yeah, it was fun. Twyla was Ariel in that production," Cassidy told Rayne.

"Here we go," Rick said then, setting down four plates in front of Rayne and Cassidy. "Let me get the coffees," he said then moved off.

I couldn't help but notice how Cassidy moved from eyeing over the desserts to eyeing over the bartender. He was definitely a dessert in and of himself, if one were so inclined. That was, of course, why I'd hired him, in addition to his mixology certificate. It never hurt to have some eye candy behind the bar. But I never expected that eye candy would fix his own eyes on me.

Cassidy nodded to herself, like she'd decided something, then turned her attention to the crème brulee. She tapped the crystalized sugar coating with the back of her spoon then scooped up a bite. She closed her eyes, sighing heavily as she ate, then said, "You have to try this." She scooped up a bite and practically shoved it into Rayne's mouth before he could protest.

"Perfect," he said between bites.

Their little exchange made that weird feeling gnaw at

my stomach again. I suddenly felt captive. I couldn't escape the scene, and as much as I wanted to not care what my friend was up to, and with whom, I did. A lot.

"How's Alice?" I asked Rayne then, shifting the conversation, shifting my attention away from the jealous feeling racking me. *Stupid. What right did I have?*

"Okay," Rayne said, suddenly looking a bit sad. "We talked after you left. He wasn't right for her. She knows it. She just wasn't expecting to get dumped like that. I don't know if she's really going to go to the ball. Well, not unless I find someone for her to go with."

"We'll both look. She needs someone fabulous," I replied.

"What about him?" Cassidy asked quietly, motioning with her spoon toward Rick. "He single? He's hot as hell. Fix her up with him."

Rayne fixed Rick with an assessing look then turned to me. "What do you think?"

"Yeah, I...I think he has someone else on his mind right now," I stammered.

"Too bad," Cassidy said with a sigh then stuck her spoon in the cherry dessert.

"Someone else on his mind, eh?" Rayne asked, his twinkly green eyes searching my face. I knew from the expression thereon that he realized I was talking about me.

"Seems like everyone has big eyes these days," I said softly then lifted a questioning eyebrow at Cassidy who was so enamored with the cherry dessert that she'd turned and started talking about it to the elderly couple sitting down the bar from us.

Rayne shook his head. "She's a friend, that's all. And what about you, Miss Hunter, and your hunky bartender? Hiring all the hot guys these days?"

"What, you looking for a job?"

He chuckled.

I shook my head. "No, he's just a friend."

"Someone quoted me a great line today: 'all things have their season.' Do you agree?" Rayne asked, setting his hand on my back, gently stroking me between my shoulder blades.

His touch felt like lightning. An intense sensation shot down to my toes, and I felt like my hair was standing on end. I looked up at him, meeting those sparkling eyes. I inhaled deeply. I caught the light honey scent that always seemed to effervesce off him. How many times had I wondered how his kiss might taste? Would it be as sweet as he smelled?

"Here we go," Rick said then, setting down the cups of coffee. I saw his eyes flick toward Rayne's hand. Rick looked away, quickly turning his attention toward Cassidy. "So, how are they?"

"Oh my god, to die for. Is the chef still here? Tell him they're awesome. Someone has some talented hands."

"Indeed," I whispered, shooting a flirty glance at Rayne.

He smiled gently at me, stroked the length of my hair.

"Okay," Cassidy said then, turning back to Rayne. "Let's chug this coffee and head out. I still need to get my van from your place. I've got sunrise yoga at the beach tomorrow morning."

"What? And leave your desserts?" Rayne asked.

"Hell no," Cassidy said, scooping up the list bite of the crème brulee. "Almost done. Just give me a sec." She then turned serious as she got to work on the last of the desserts.

Once again, jealousy shot through me. Why was her vehicle at his farm? Where had they been?

Rayne sipped his coffee and looked over my scattered mess of books and notes. "So after your degree, then what?"

"Assuming I finish, we'll see. I need to pass this test first," I replied, looking back at my book. I was also mindful of the note lying to the side of my papers about Monsieur Beaumont, yet another duty I still had to attend to.

"You'll be fine. I've never seen you fail at anything."

"Well, the harder I work, the luckier I get. And I do tend to get what I want."

"Of course you do. You've got beauty, brains, and you're a hard worker. And besides, who could ever resist those eyes of yours?"

"Me? I'm not the one with the sparkle."

"You have plenty of sparkle."

"Done!" Cassidy announced.

Rayne chuckled then pulled out his wallet.

"On the house," I told him, setting my hand on his.

He shook his head. "Don't want to set a precedent. By the way, that crème brulee really needed some organic honey, don't you think?" he said, turning to Cassidy as he set a bill on the bar.

"Definitely. But otherwise, it was kinda like the food of the gods."

I nodded to Rayne. "I'll be sure to order some. Need to find a reputable vendor first, not some kooky hippie."

"Of course not. Don't want those types around," Rayne said with a good-natured laugh then slipped off his seat. "Catch you tomorrow?"

I smiled. "Hope so. I'm packed up with stuff, but I'm sure I'll see you around," I said, knowing full well that seeing Rayne was something I always managed to juggle into my schedule, not that he needed to know that. I turned to his friend. "Nice to meet you, Cassidy."

"You too," she said then turned to Rick. "Night!"

From the glass washing stand, he nodded to them. "Goodnight."

Rayne shot me the softest of smiles, winked at me, then headed out behind Cassidy.

All I could do was stare at the door after they'd gone.

A few minutes later, I heard the click of a glass on the bar in front of me. I looked back to realize Rick had set out two shot glasses, one for him and one for me. Wordlessly, he poured us both a whiskey. He lifted the glass and motioned for me to do the same.

"Here's to sizing up the competition," he said with a wink.

I couldn't help by laugh. Indeed. I couldn't tell if Cassidy was really my competition or not, but she sure seemed to know more about Rayne than I did. And I hated it. And I hated that I hated it. I suspected that Rick was feeling the same way about Rayne that I was feeling about Cassidy, about which I felt very sorry. But what could I do? After all, Rayne hadn't actually taken anything beyond flirtation and a vibe. You couldn't count on a vibe. I sighed then lifted my glass. "Cheers," I said then, clicking glasses with him.

At that, we both drank. And as the warm liquid slid down my throat, I couldn't help but close my eyes once more and dream about honey-sweetened kisses.

rayne

The bees hummed softly as I approached the row of straw bee skeps sitting alongside the back wall of my barn.

"Good morning," I called to them.

A few of the workers buzzed around me excitedly. While we faeries looked like humans, we had skills beyond the reach of most mortals. Speaking to the natural world came quite easily. Even when I was a young boy, I had a special affinity for speaking with winged creatures: bees, butterflies, birds, dragonflies. As it turned out, the bees and I understood one another best.

I chuckled good-naturedly then listened.

"In Chancellor?" I asked as they told me about a man they had spotted who had a glow that matched Alice's. The bees could see each person's aura, the colorful magnetic hue that surrounded people, and every person had a vibrational match. Finally, they'd spotted someone who was right for my girl.

I nodded as they shared their last bit of intel: "Lavender Fields Bed and Breakfast. Well, then I guess it's time to make a call on Genevieve. Surely her guests need some honey with their morning tea. Have anything for me?"

The bees rushed off to one of the skeps that was positively glowing with golden light.

"Pardon me," I said politely as I set my hand on the little straw dome.

With that, the bees left the straw hive, flying like a torrent out of the little straw skep. The queen was the last to exit.

"Your majesty," I said, inclining my head. "I'll be just a moment."

She turned and flew off to join the others.

I gently lifted the straw skep. Pulling an old bone tool from my back pocket, I removed the honey-laden combs, setting them into a well-worn wooden collecting tray. When I was done, I returned the skep to its upright position.

Most of the bees had gone back to work in the apple orchard. I gazed at the trees. The orchard was a beautiful sight, row after row of apple trees loaded in pink and white blossoms. Dandelions, forget-me-nots, and new violets sprang up like a watercolor patchwork under the lovely canopy. I loved spring in Chancellor. I hoped Ziggy was right, that when my work was done, I would be able to stay. And not just for the view.

"All done. Bright blessings and many thanks to you," I called to the bees, then went to the barn with the honeycombs.

Once inside, I grabbed my wooden uncapping tool. Working quickly, I uncapped the wax, revealing the amber-colored honey underneath. Dabbing the honey with my finger, I took a taste. The sweet flavor filled my mouth. I could taste an undertone of apple in the honey. Once all the combs were uncapped, I dropped them into the honey extractor and turned it on. In no time, the honey was ready. I filled up a dozen jars, mindful to slip some fresh honeycomb into the old mason jars as Genevieve preferred. She wanted her guests to know they had authentic honey on their breakfast table. I then washed up and got ready to go.

I was filled with excitement. Finally, a guy for Alice. The bees didn't know who the man was, only that he'd only arrived in Chancellor that morning. But they did have one other interesting bit of information. He'd come to the bed and breakfast in a car owned by Blushing Grape Vineyards. It seemed that everywhere I turned,

Viola's family was in my life. Surely, that meant something.

What mattered most, however, was Alice's happiness. And for the first time in a long time, we were on to something. All things had their season. Finally, it was Alice's time.

I PULLED MY OLD TRUCK INTO THE PARKING LOT of Lavender Fields Bed and Breakfast just after lunch. It was warm for a spring day, and I saw that the first of Genevieve's lavenders were blooming. The field next to the Victorian mansion, which was painted the same hue as the flower whose name it bore, was alive with purplish blue flowers. The owner of the bed and breakfast was on the porch watering hanging baskets.

I grabbed the box of honey off the seat. The cardboard box from Tess' shop was still sitting there. I needed to remember to take it into the house. Lord knows what other treasures Cassidy had missed, and I needed to get those tools cleaned up.

"Hey, Rayne," Genevieve called from the front porch. Setting down her watering can, she wiped her hands on her apron. In her early fifties, Genevieve had moved to Chancellor around the same time I'd arrived. She was unique, capturing my interest from the start. Most women at least noticed my faerie sparkle, but she barely looked at me. The reason, however, was far from magical. Over time, she'd opened up to me just a little, telling me of a bad marriage which had an even worse end. She'd seen the old Victorian for sale online and decided to come to Chancellor to start a new life. Each time I saw her, I could see her heart was slowly stitching itself back together. But she was still a wounded thing. It was strange what humans did to one another. Faeries never treated each other so roughly, especially not in matters of the heart. Maybe it's because we knew what delicate organs hearts really were, both physically and energetically. It saddened me to see her in such a state, a perpetually broken thing. Many times I wondered where her fairy godparent was. Next time I saw Ziggy, I would ask about Genevieve.

"Thought you might be running low," I told her as I carried the box up the stairs.

"Good guess. It's getting busy. Spring is here again, and with the lavender starting to bloom, I'm booking up early. Come on in," she said.

Genevieve had restored the Victorian mansion back to its original splendor. Brocade wallpaper, elaborate moulding, shimmering wood floors covered with ornate Turkish rugs, and period furniture decorated the place. A massive wooden staircase at the center of the house divided the space in half. On the left was a lovely parlor painted in pale purple and decorated with charming period chaises, sofas, and even an elaborate birdcage from which two sparrows called to me.

Hello. Hello.

I whistled back to them.

Genevieve smiled. "How do they always know it's you?"

"The honey. I must smell good," I replied, following her to the right where a second parlor, which had been turned into a dining room, adjoined the more formal dining space.

"If you say so, but they only do that with you. How odd. So, how many do you have?" she asked, looking into the crate.

"Dozen."

She nodded. "I'll go grab some cash if you'd like to grab the empties off the tables," she said then headed back to the kitchen.

There were two couples finishing up lunch and a single gentleman sipping tea while he read over some papers. I set about picking up the old jars of honey while I assessed the options. Both couples were older and very much *coupled*. No luck there. The young man sitting with his papers, however, seemed like a good bet. And there was something about him, a certain shine, which told me he was the one. My gut confirmed it, urging me to say hello. It was the same feeling I'd experienced the day I'd met Horatio's would-be girlfriend, Julie. I'd seen Julie walking down the street among a busy crowd and in that singular moment, I knew there was something special about her. And there was. For one, she turned out to be a pretty talented hearth witch. And for two, she was my best friend's true love. I'd learned along the way, that when it came to patching up couples, I had good instincts.

"Pardon me?" I said politely as I approached the man. "May I take that jar if you are finished with it?"

The man looked up at me from over the rim of his glasses. I could see I had distracted him from his thoughts. He wasn't upset, just surprised. I eyed him over. He had wavy reddish-brown hair and brown eyes. Surely handsome enough for Alice.

"*Je m'excuse*," he said politely. "Sorry. Excuse me. I was distracted. Of course."

French. He was French? While his English was perfect, there was no missing the accent.

I nodded and carefully lifted the jar as I glanced at his

papers. Thereon, I saw a number of equations and charts. "In town on business?"

The man nodded and gave me a friendly smiled. "*Oui*. There is a conference at the college tomorrow. Just, eh, familiarizing, myself with my presentation."

"Your first time in Chancellor?" I asked, trying to amp up some of my faerie sparkle.

He nodded. "In Chancellor, yes. You're from here? Please..." he said, motioning to the seat across from him.

Bingo. "Thanks," I said, joining him. "I'm just waiting on Genevieve," I added, tapping the empty jar.

"The honey? Very nice. It has a very sweet aroma. You must have apples."

"How did you know?"

The man tapped his nose. "Trained. I'm Luc," he said then, reaching out to shake my hand.

"Rayne," I replied, returning the gesture. "Trained?"

"My family...perfumers. We have factories near the lavender fields in Provence. As I was telling Miss Harper," he said, referring to Genevieve. "I feel right at home here," he said with a smile.

Okay. Great. He was smart, handsome, and friendly... all good for Alice. But he was from another country. How was that ever going to work? "That's Chancellor for you. I've lived all over, but there is something very special about this place."

Luc nodded, but I saw a sad shadow cross his face. There was a longing behind his eyes. Something told me that the idea of traveling around until he found some place he wanted to live was quite outside his grasp. I knew the look. Horatio used to have the same shadow behind his eyes. It was the look of a man trapped by his good fortune.

"Here you go," Genevieve said then, returning from the back. She handed me an envelope. "Ah, I see you've met Monsieur Beaumont."

"We were just getting acquainted," I replied.

Genevieve smiled then peered over our heads out the window. "Out of time, I'm afraid. Looks like your ride is here, monsieur," she said, then cast a glance toward the door.

We both turned to hear the front door open. A moment later, the sparrows called to me.

She's coming. She's coming.

A second later, Viola Hunter turned the corner.

The moment her eyes settled on me, my heart felt like it had been filled with liquid sunlight. All I wanted to do was race across the room, sweep her into my arms, and plant a kiss on her lips. If only...

CHAPTER 8

viola

"Rayne?" *Now what in the world was he doing here?*

"Hi, Viola," he said, grinning at me like *that* again.

The man seated with Rayne stood. "Mademoiselle Hunter?"

I looked at him. Who in the world was this guy? Maybe he was traveling with Monsieur Beaumont? He was far too young, and way too hot, to be the guy whose photo I'd seen on the Beaumont company webpage.

"Yes. I...I'm here to take Monsieur Beau—"

The stranger flashed me a charming smile. "I am Monsieur Beaumont," he said, then chuckled. "I see you were expecting my father."

Blowing it, Viola. Need to put on some Cinderella-style charm stat. "*Pardonnez-moi,* monsieur. Yes, admittedly, I thought I was supposed to meet your father. Professor Wallace asked me to bring you over to the college for a meeting this afternoon. My assistant phoned you?"

He nodded. "Yes, just let me gather my things."

"I hope you aren't feeling too jet-lagged," I said. Surely, Professor Wallace realized the man might need some sleep.

"Not at all. I slept on the plane," he replied as he stowed his papers into a briefcase.

"Oh, and I have something for you as well," I said, turning my attention to Genevieve. "Judy said you hadn't been by to pick up Lavender Fields' tickets for the Cherry Blossom Ball. I brought them along."

"Thank you, Viola. That was very kind of you, but I don't think..."

I pressed the tickets toward her. "Do come."

"I hardly have a thing to wear."

"New dress shop in town, right Rayne?" I said, angling to get some help. Genevieve was the most successful lodging proprietor in Chancellor, but she rarely participated in social events. I liked the woman. There were a lot of people in town who could help her if she just socialized a bit more. The ball, which most of the chamber of commerce members attended, would be the perfect chance to get her out and about.

"There is. New designer. She just opened a place on Main Street by The Glass Mermaid."

"Threaded Bliss Bridal Boutique," I added.

"That's the place," Rayne said.

Genevieve smiled shyly. "I'll think about it."

"And you...Julie said you didn't answer her text," I told Rayne then, referring to the conversation I'd had an hour earlier with my brother's girlfriend.

"Julie sent a text?" Rayne replied, confused. He pulled out his phone. "Ah. Dead battery."

"I swear, why do you even carry that thing? You never have it charged."

"I can tell the time by the slant of the sun and placement of the stars. Who needs a cell phone?"

"You know it does more than tell time, right?"

Rayne chuckled. "What's up?"

"Barbeque at SerendipiTEA Gardens tonight. Six o'clock. Not sure what that equates to in rays of the sun," I told him with a wink.

"That's what time the sun sets over the lake," Rayne replied, matter of factly.

"Really? I never noticed."

"Well, that sounds like something I need to remedy."

"Is that so?" The image of Rayne and me walking hand in hand along the beach at sunset gripped me with such a feverish desire that I had to force myself to focus. "Sounds... perfect. But for now..." I said then turned my gaze back to the startlingly young and handsome Monsieur Beaumont who was grinning at Rayne and me. "Monsieur, are you ready?"

"*Oui*, but I didn't dare interrupt. I wanted to see how it would turn out," he said then looked at Rayne. "Well done," he told him with a wink.

Rayne grinned then stuck out his hand. "Nice to meet you, Luc," he said then turned to me. "Is Luc's schedule full? Perhaps he'd enjoy an American-style barbeque and some pleasant company."

There was a glint in Rayne's eye, not the usual sparkle that lived there, but something more mischievous. What did he have up his sleeve?

"I don't believe so. I'll check with Professor Wallace. If you aren't busy this evening, perhaps you'd like to join us?"

"*Merci*. Of course," Luc replied.

I couldn't help but notice Rayne grinning happily. He then turned to Genevieve. "And you, Ms. Harper? How about a night off?"

Genevieve shifted nervously. "I have so much to do here. The house is full. The dinner rush..."

"Come after. The food will be amazing. The company even better," I told her.

She smiled. "If I have a chance."

"Monsieur Beaumont," I said then, motioning toward the door. Fully aware that I had a chemistry test tomorrow morning, the last thing I wanted to do was piss off Professor Wallace by running late. "Call Julie," I told Rayne.

"Will do. Drive carefully," he said with a wave.

With that, we headed outside. The scent of lavender drifted across the field, perfuming the wind. I stopped and inhaled deeply. "Spanish lavender," I said absently.

"*Oui*. Good nose," Luc said as he slipped into the car.

"Thank you. My family...we try to incorporate local ingredients in our fruit wines. We've used some of Ms. Harper's lavender before. My nose is trained on the grape, but it has higher aspirations."

"So Professor Wallace mentioned."

"Nosing the wine is one of my specialties, but I'd like to move into your trade one day."

"Perfumery?"

I nodded.

"No better place to study than in France."

"Perhaps, once I'm done with my degree."

"We offer an apprenticeship program over the

summer. It's a very exclusive program, but Professor Wallace spoke highly of your academics."

I tried to hide the excitement that shot through me like a lightning bolt. But a moment after I considered it, I knew it was impossible. Dad was back at the helm, but I was still needed at the restaurant, and France was so far from....everyone. "Sounds like an amazing opportunity."

"It is. But it's only for people with a good nose."

"Well, I'll put on my best Cyrano de Bergerac then."

Luc smiled, and we drove up the hill toward the college. All the while, my mind was busy playing out the dream of me walking through French lavender fields dreaming up the next Chanel No. 5. And for some reason, in that fantasy, I couldn't shake the image of Rayne walking at my side.

rayne

"Rayne!" Horatio Hunter called happily when I pulled into the parking lot of Green Earth Apothecary and SerendipiTEA Gardens. Behind the shop was a small garden area that Julie, the shop owner and Horatio's girlfriend, had transformed into the perfect backyard terrace, complete with a brick grill which Horatio was manning. Julie, her red hair shimmering in the dimming sunlight, was covering a long, butcher-block outdoor table with a flower-print tablecloth. She waved to us.

"We're late," Alice scolded as she hopped out of the truck.

I glanced at the setting sun. "No, we aren't."

"Maybe I'm just hungry," she said with a laugh.

"You do own a restaurant, you know."

"Shut up."

Chuckling, I stuffed my hands into my pockets and followed Alice onto the terrace. The smell of burning hickory wafted up from the grill where Horatio was stoking the fire.

"Hey, Rayne," Julie called happily as she pulled Alice into a hug.

"Grab me a couple of logs, would you?" Horatio said to me, pointing toward the firewood piled neatly nearby.

Grabbing the wood, I wondered for the five-hundredth time what, exactly, Horatio would think if I started to...or even wanted to...date Viola. Before Julie moved to Chancellor, Horatio and I used to hit local scene in search of fun. But that's all it had been. Fun. Viola, well, that was something different. Would he understand? While I'd always found Viola beautiful, and the flirty conversation was always amusing, I wanted something more. My feelings for Viola had become more serious. I hoped that with Julie in the picture, maybe Horatio would be cool about me breaking "bro code." But first I needed to worry about Alice. As long as Viola brought Luc tonight, things would start moving in the right direction. Perhaps destiny would just take its course. And if not, I had my wand hidden inside my pocket.

I handed the wood to Horatio while I eyed over the selection that Julie, whose baking skills only slightly surpassed her cooking skills, had set out. Plates of marinating portabella mushrooms and veggie shishkabobs waited.

"Looks amazing, Julie," I told her, letting my nose sniff out just what Julie had used to marinate the food. Julie's skills in the kitchen were a product of her own talent, of course, but it didn't hurt that she was a gifted kitchen witch. It wasn't like she announced it to the world, but Julie had joined Chancellor's coven of good witches shortly after moving here. According to the elders, witches had lived in Chancellor since the town's beginning. I could see them, and they were always quick to notice my sparkle, but I was pretty sure they didn't know what I was. I wanted to keep it like that. After all, I wasn't the only sparkly "other" in Chancellor. You didn't have to talk to Kate, the owner of the little boutique called The Glass Mermaid, for more than a few minutes without noticing that she was...different. Her voice was more melodious and soothing than the average person, her shimmer beyond compare. I long suspected she might be better-suited to a life under the waves than above them, but I never shared my thoughts with anyone. What did it matter to me, a faerie, if a mermaid also walked among the humans in Chancellor?

"Man, no steaks? Burgers?" Alice said as she handed me a beer.

"Of course. They are inside in the fridge," Julie said coming up behind us as she looked over the fire. "How long, my dear?" she asked Horatio.

"Just a few more minutes," he replied, pausing to kiss her on the forehead.

"Give me a hand?" Julie asked Alice.

"Sure. You make a dessert? I'm still eating through my misery."

"Of course! Old recipe. Mrs. Row gave it to me. Strawberries, cream cheese, and pretzels," Julie was saying as they walked inside.

"Sounds weird," Alice commented.

I chuckled. I'd bet money it was *wyrd* for sure.

I watched Horatio as his eyes followed Julie inside.

"A man in love," I told him, lifting my bottle. "To love."

Horatio lifted his drink. "To love," he said, tapping his bottle against mine.

"How go the plans for the ball?" I asked. Horatio, who had recently extricated himself from his father's business, was working with the arts council on planning the upcoming Cherry Blossom Ball.

"Well, I need this beer, that's for sure. But it's coming together. Man...I need to tell you something. I have something special planned for the ball...for Julie," he said, casting a nervous glance behind him.

"Do tell."

"I'm going to ask her...I'm going to ask her to marry me."

A weird feeling swept across my stomach, a strange mixture of excited happiness and jealously. My reaction startled me.

"Congrats, man," I said, patting him on the back. I took a sip of the beer, clearing my throat which had suddenly gone dry. "Tell Viola yet?"

Horatio shook his head. "She's been busy with school and is just distracted. I think she's getting ready to cut ties with the company. She's all over the place."

"Regardless, brother, you better tell her or she'll be furious at you."

"Will do. Still need to break it to my dad. That should be fun. Ah, speaking of Viola," Horatio said then, nodding over my shoulder.

I turned to see Viola and Luc crossing the parking lot toward us. God, she looked beautiful. The sunset shimmered on her hair, making it glimmer with glints of blue and gold. She laughed politely as Luc spoke to her. Once more, my stomach twisted.

"Well, that's interesting. I thought he was supposed to be some old scientist guy. He knows that's my sister, I hope," Horatio said then waved to the pair.

Viola smiled at me.

I waved to Luc. "Welcome! Beer or wine?"

"Let's have a beer," Luc replied.

"Luc, this is my brother, Horatio," Viola introduced as I headed over to the cooler.

"Horatio...I've not heard this name before. Is it common?" Luc asked.

Horatio laughed good-naturedly. It wasn't the first time someone questioned him about his name. "No. Viola and I...our mother was very into the theater. She named us for characters in Shakespeare plays. Horatio was a character in *Hamlet*. Mom picked the name because the Horatio in the play was an honest man and a good friend. His honesty kept him out of trouble."

"And Viola?" Luc asked.

"From *Twelfth Night*. She wins the love of a duke."

Luc laughed. "Those are in short supply these days."

"Who. Is. That?" Alice asked as she sidled up beside me, her eyes fixed on Luc.

At that same moment, one of my honey bees whisked by, a buzzing whisper refocusing me on the real reason why I was there. I wasn't there for Viola or Horatio...I was there for Alice. And right now, I needed to pay attention.

"Let me introduce you," I said with a grin, taking the massive bowl of some delicious-looking fruit salad from her hands and handing her two bottles of beer which she took absently from me.

"Dammit. I'm a mess," Alice whispered. "Why didn't you tell me a hot guy was going to be here? I look like crap."

I scanned her quickly. She was dressed casual, jeans and a T-shirt with the deli logo on it, her hair pulled back in a ponytail. She looked perfectly fine, natural in her beauty, but she was also right. I should have warned her. I was terrible at this. And there was no way I could just whip out my wand and *bibbidi-bobbidi-boo* her into a sparkling blue gown. If there was a prize for worst fairy godfather on the planet, I was definitely going to win.

"Luc," I called, directing Alice toward him. "Let me introduce you to our friend. This is Alice."

"*Enchanté*," he said, smiling at her.

I couldn't help but see him scan her face, his eyes assessing. And after a moment, I saw the slight lift at the corners of his mouth. Clearly, despite her casual attire, he liked what he saw. And, I was pleased to see, it was just her face he'd scanned...nothing below the chin. Now, that was a gentleman.

Alice giggled. Like, full-on giggled, which made Viola raise an eyebrow at her.

"Beer?" she said, handing him the bottle.

Oh good lord. I cast a desperate glance at Viola. My eyes screaming *help*.

Viola nodded.

"Alice is a business owner," Viola told Luc. "She owns a little deli downtown."

"Bagels," Alice explained. Suddenly looking embarrassed, she added, "Oh, I do make croissant too. Bagels aren't the only breakfast pastry in the world that's good. I mean, they're good but—"

"I love bagels," Luc interrupted. "Don't tell my countrymen, but I always grab one when I have a layover in New York. Is that correct, that they make the best bagels?"

Alice relaxed and sipped her beer. "It's the way they are made. New York bagels are the most authentic. You have to boil them to get the right texture," she started explaining just as Julie came out of the back of the shop carrying two large platters.

"Help?" Julie called.

I cast a glance at glance at Luc and Alice. To my surprise, Luc was listening to her with rapt attention.

"Coming," Viola called, motioning for me to follow her. "Did you see that?" Viola whispered.

"See what?" I asked with a smirk.

"Oh my god, shut up. You saw it too. The little, I don't know, moment."

"I saw it," Horatio said, coming up behind us.

"Rebounds can be good. He's a nice guy. Very polite," Viola said.

Horatio took one tray from Julie. When I reached out for the other, she handed it instead to Viola.

"Help me with something?" Julie said, motioning for me to come inside with her.

I nodded and followed her.

Julie's bracelets jangled as she grabbed two glasses off a tray sitting on the counter inside. Julie's little shop was at the front of the house. At the back was her small apartment. She handed the glasses to me. "New recipe. Super healthy. Thought you and Viola might like them," she said with a smile.

I looked at the slender glasses, smelling rose petals, honey, mint...and something else. But more, I could see a certain glow around the drinks. Many of Julie's dishes carried the hint of magic with them. And I knew for certain that this kitchen witch knew which way my heart leaned. I smiled at her then shook my head. "Not yet. All things have their season...but thank you."

She sighed heavily. "Why don't you just tell her?"

"Is it so obvious?"

"To me."

"And what about Horatio?"

"Clueless."

I chuckled. "I think, perhaps, there might be a better mark for these," I said, casting a glance at the drinks. "And I could use some help."

"Could you, Mr. Twinkly Eyes?"

I grinned at her but said nothing. While I knew Julie was a witch, she still didn't know about me.

"Okay, okay. Don't tell me," she said with a smile. "Fine."

"Later."

"Later?"

"Much later."

Julie laughed. "I'm going to hold you to it."

"It's a promise. But later. Jules, about Horatio, do you think he'd be okay with Viola and—"

"...and you? Not sure, but that is something I *can* help you with."

"Thank you."

"You so owe me."

"I know."

"Alice," Julie called, hoisting the drinks in the direction of my girl and her new friend. "Try this? And Luc, right? I'm Julie," she said, deftly taking the beers from their hands, replacing them with what I was very certain were love potions.

I sat down in one of lounge chairs and watched as Alice and Luc sipped their drinks and compared notes about cuisine.

Julie turned, winked at me, then headed over to the grill.

Viola sat down in the chaise beside me. She sighed heavily. "I should be studying. I'm going to fail my chemistry test tomorrow," she said, clicking her bottle of beer against mine. "But right now, I don't care." She glanced at Alice and Luc then leaned in toward me. "Looks promising."

So close to me, I could smell the sweet scent of vanilla perfuming her hair. I closed my eyes and inhaled in a subtle, not-too-stalkerish way. She smelled beautiful. I slid my hand down her arm, slipping my hand into hers. "Yes, it does," I whispered.

Viola paused for a moment then turned and looked at me. Her eyes met mine then she searched my face, as if to determine if I was playing with her. When she realized my sincerity, she smiled softly. "Curiouser and curiouser," she said.

"How so?"

"Your eyes aren't twinkling now. Why not?"

"You're the expert on chemistry. You tell me." Cautiously, I lifted her hand and placed the softest kiss thereon.

Viola grinned. "Well, that escalated quickly," she said, but I could see she was breathing hard, her humor masking her true feelings.

"Too quickly?"

She shook her head. "Not fast enough."

"Well, we'll have to remedy that then," I said then gazed quickly at the others. Alice and Luc were fully engrossed with one another, Alice laughing at some joke he'd made. Working at the grill, Julie cast a glance over her shoulder. She winked at me then wrapped her arm around Horatio, ensuring his attention was fully on her.

When I looked back at Viola, I saw that she was looking at me. She also stole a quick glance toward her brother who wasn't paying her any attention, then leaned toward me and set a soft kiss on my lips.

If I had real faerie wings, surely they would have melted off. Her lips were as warm and soft as I had imagined, and the light taste of beer mixed with a sweet, sugary taste flavored her kiss. I was overcome with her scent of vanilla as again I drank from those lips.

Finally.

Finally.

Viola.

A moment later, she pulled away and sighed heavily.

I breathed heavily and pulled her close to me, pressing my cheek against her head.

"Who is hungry?" Horatio called then moved to turn.

Like two guilty things, Viola and I pulled away from one another, quite nearly caught.

"What?" Horatio asked, clearly perplexed by the unusual expression on our faces.

"You aren't cooking, are you?" Viola covered quickly.

"Wouldn't dream of it."

"Then sure," she said, sticking out her tongue at him.

Viola lifted her beer bottle once more then leaned against me as I put my arm around her.

"Let's do that again some time," she said.

"Agreed."

"Like, a lot."

"Preferably," I replied.

"Soon."

"Soon," I answered, feeling very certain my heart had just exploded with joy.

viola

Professor Wallace's teaching assistant was more engrossed with texting than bothering to see if anyone was cheating. Some proctor she was. It only annoyed me because my phone had been buzzing for the last ten minutes, and I couldn't check it in the middle of an exam. I was almost done, but still, what if it was Rayne?

Rayne.

Rayne had kissed me.

Well, no, that wasn't exactly right. Rayne had kissed my hand. I had turned and full-on sucked his face off. But he had kissed me back. And more than that, I'd finally gotten a kind of admission out of him. From what I could tell, he wanted me just as much as I wanted him.

Focus, Viola.

Forcing myself to finish the last question, I quickly went back through and checked my work. It looked like all my answers were right, the test having been much easier than I'd expected.

Gathering my things, I left the test with the TA then headed out of the classroom.

I pulled out my phone. Luc's presentation started in fifteen minutes. I could make it. As I rushed toward the auditorium, I scrolled through my messages: Judy from work, the restaurant, Horatio wanted me to call him ASAP, and Alice texting me furiously about Luc. Apparently he'd accepted an invitation to have dinner with Alice and her friends, Kate and Cooper. Something must have been in the air last night. Alice and Luc had hit it off and were still sitting in front of the fire chatting when I finally went home. Horatio assured me he'd see to it that Luc either got back to the B & B or had somewhere to sleep. I didn't know where he'd ended up.

Quietly, I slipped into the back of the auditorium just as the last speaker was finishing up. Luc, who looked tired but happy, was waiting to present next.

I looked through my phone once more.

No messages from Rayne.

No reason to worry, right? I mean, it was Rayne, after all. It wasn't like he was going anywhere, and he wasn't, as near as I could tell, playing. He wouldn't do that to me. I was sure of it.

Luc is about to present. I'm on campus, I messaged to Alice. *How late were you guys up?*

Well, I saw the sunrise... ;)

Oh! Lol. Saw it from the beach or...

Or...

Alice! No wonder he looks so happy.

Does he? He called me twice already today. That's not too stalker-like, is it?

No. He's a nice guy.

From France.

Yeah, from France. He's going to present now. Need to put the phone down.

Send a pic! Pleeeeease?

Working discreetly, I took a quick picture of Luc standing at the podium. Apparently he'd made it back to the B & B at some point because he was dressed in a nicely-pressed suit. I sent the photo to Alice.

A moment later, she replied. *Best rebound ever. Later.*

I turned off my phone and tuned my attention to the front of the room. I pulled out my notepad. Luc described his family's perfume making methods and how one of his small farms in Provence was experimenting with antique distillation methods, using organic ingredients, and getting better oils and stronger scents. As I noted the fine points of Luc's presentation, I also started listing out the combination of herbals I wanted to try. Everything I needed grew in Chancellor. Our old distillery could easily be transformed into a boutique perfumery. But I needed more hands-on experience, exactly the kind of experience Luc's summer apprenticeship offered. But now what? This wasn't the right time to leave. I mean, after all, Rayne and I had finally kissed. This *was* the right time to start a relationship, not running off to study flowers.

I sat listening to Luc, rapt by his discussion of his work. I felt an odd swelling in my chest. Luc was living the life I wanted, pursuing my dream. One summer wasn't too long, was it? Rayne was always so chill. Would he be like that in a relationship or was I making too much of that kiss?

After Luc's presentation, I slipped down the row to congratulate him while a group of Japanese scholars prepared to present.

"Well done," I whispered, sliding into the seat beside him.

He smiled at me. God, he looked truly happy. His glow...it was more than just a one-night-stand kind of glow. "*Merci.* I hope it got you thinking a bit more about that apprenticeship I mentioned?"

"Yes. I'd love to do it. I just need to talk to my...family.

Speaking of which, I need to get going for a bit. Can I do anything for you?"

Luc shook his head. "*Non*, I'll be at the symposium for a while longer then have an appointment with President White. Oh, tonight Alice arranged for her and me to have dinner. You didn't have any plans for me, did you?"

I grinned. "Even if I did, I'd cancel them in a heartbeat. Have a great time with Alice. Do you have the number for my assistant?"

He nodded. "And for a car, if needed. Thank you, Viola."

"Of course. You're in town until Sunday, right?"

"*Oui*."

"There is a dance, a ball actually, tomorrow night. Horatio is organizing the event. Would you like to come?"

"Will Alice be there?"

I smiled. "Yes. And I believe she needs an escort. I'll make sure you have a ticket and a tuxedo."

"Please, if it's not too much trouble."

"Not at all. Okay then," I said, patting him on the shoulder. "See you tomorrow night."

He nodded, smiling.

I slipped out as the next lecture began.

Pulling out my cell, I sent a quick text to Alice. *You have a date for the ball. And you're welcome.*

No way? He'll go?

I'm even going to get him a tux. Have fun tonight.

Girl, please.

I chuckled then dialed Horatio's number. He picked up right away.

"Hey, what's up?" I asked.

"You free? I was kinda hoping I could get you and Dad together. I want to talk to you both about something," he replied.

"Everything okay?"

"Perfect. Can you join us out at the winery?"

"Sure. Wait, are you already out there? Why aren't you working?"

"I…I took the afternoon off. You're coming now?"

"I'll be there in fifteen."

"Good. See you then."

Okay, what in the world was going on?

I glanced at my phone and debated. Still unsure, and frustrated with myself for my apprehension, I dialed Rayne's number. We were, after all, still friends. And I knew Rayne. He might have played around in the past, but he wasn't going to do that to me. It just wasn't his style.

I was surprised, and more than a little annoyed, to hear a female voice answer his phone. "Hello."

I looked at the phone, thinking for a moment I had

dialed the wrong number. Nope, it was Rayne's line. "Hello?"

"Oh! Viola, right?" the girl said. "Your name popped up on the screen."

"Yeah. I...I was looking for Rayne."

"He's tied up. You need him urgently? I can probably get him."

"Who is this?"

"Sorry, it's Cassidy."

Who the hell was this girl, and what was she doing with Rayne—again? "Um. No. Just tell him I called?"

"Will do."

"Okay. Thanks," I said then hung up.

Blood boiling, I shoved my phone back in my bag. What in the hell was Rayne playing at? And who was that girl? Family friend, eh? Well, at that very moment I was glad that I was on my way to see my big brother, because right then, I needed to talk to someone who might have an explanation or Horatio needed to punch Rayne in the face.

rayne

"W ell?" I asked, looking at Cassidy who was sitting in the lotus position on the bench outside the fitting room.

"It's frumpy. And odd. You look like a wedding singer...from the eighties."

The tuxedo rental salesman frowned at her.

"Well, he does. We're looking for James Bond, not Kevin James. Try again."

"I can spend a bit more, if you have something a little nicer," I told the man.

"Dude, think about who you are trying to impress. Bring out the big guns," Cassidy told me.

I nodded in assent. "Your best tux," I told the little man who scampered away. Cassidy was right. I needed to show Viola I wasn't just a hippie farmer. I was worthy of being at her side.

"Oh! Speaking of, guess who called," Cassidy said then, waggling my phone at me.

I took it from her hand to see that Viola had called while I was wiggling in and out what seemed like an endless line of ill-fitting suits. "No message," I muttered aloud.

"Nah, I answered it. Told her you were tied up."

"You answered my phone?"

She nodded then pulled out her own cell. "Crap. Twyla called too. I need to call her back, and I'm getting late," she said then rose, gathering up her things.

"Wait, what did Viola say?"

"Uh...just to tell you she called. So, don't cheap out on the tux, all right?"

I nodded. "Thanks for your help." Cassidy and I didn't spend a lot of time together, but when we did, there was a certain kinship between us. It was nice to be around someone who knew what I was. She was, undoubtedly, pretty, but not my taste. She was too fey, never taking life too seriously. I wanted someone with more drive, someone like Viola.

"Welcome! Oh, got a lead on a prom date. Fencing lessons. Skyla was right. There's a real prospect there.

Nice kid. Good family. Just one swish of the wand, and I'll be all set."

I laughed. "Well done."

"And you?"

"We found Alice a Frenchman."

"You and your bees. I need to get some bees."

"You do great with your wand. I was never any good at it."

With that, Cassidy pulled out the long silver pin that was holding her hair into a bun. The single hair pin looked like nothing fancy at first glance, but on closer inspection, one could see that the silver had an extra special shimmer, and the jewel on the eye of the swan figure at the top of the pin glimmered unusually.

"You just need practice," she said then gave her wand a wave. I saw the air around her shimmer as she chanted:

Like a glove, let it fit
With weeds of black across his hip
And may Viola see delight
In Rayne's eyes tomorrow night

The glimmering light from Cassidy's wand sparkled all around me then traveled out of the dressing room toward the shop.

A moment later, we both heard the little salesman exclaim, "Ah-ha! I know just the one!"

"We aren't supposed to use it on one another," I whispered, feeling grateful all the same.

"What, you gonna tell on me? You owe me one. See ya," she said then, sticking her wand back into her mound of hair. With a wave, she headed out of the little shop.

"Here we are. Let's try this one," the salesman said, returning with yet another suit. This time, however, I could see just from the look of the fabric that Cassidy's spell had worked. "I forgot I had this one. It came in a few weeks back, and I was planning to return it to the company. But I think this will do the trick," he said, leading me back into the dressing room.

Setting the phone aside for a moment, I followed the little man. More than anything, I wanted Viola to walk into the ball on my arm feeling happy, confident, and appreciated. If a simple suit could help to show her that, then it was easily done. I would do anything to make her happy.

CHAPTER 12

viola

I parked my car in the winery parking lot just as Jessica, the tasting room hostess, escorted a small group outside. They were making their way to Roger, our wine educator, who was waiting at the edge of the vineyard. The tasting tours were already getting busy. Genevieve was right; spring was hopping this year.

"They're back by the Chancellors," Jessica called to me, referring to the section of the vineyard where we grew our signature Chancellor grapes.

I slipped off my heels, trading them for the pair of work boots that I always kept in the trunk, then headed into the vineyard. Since it was early spring, chartreuse-colored leaves were uncurling on the vines. While I'd never had any formal education in viticulture, I knew my vines. I'd grown up in the vineyard, chasing Horatio through row after row of grapes, our mother singing show toons as she tracked us down, our father grumbling under his breath. While things were better now, both Horatio and I had grown up feeling like an inconvenience to our father. I must have been in my teens when I stopped caring what my dad thought. As long as I smiled, minded my manners, and did what I was told, Dad was happy. Over time, I'd steeled myself to Dad's moods. What did I care if he was disappointed in me? He was always disappointed in someone. When Mom died, Dad hit rock bottom, becoming a total bastard. Around Halloween, however, everything had changed. For the first time in our lives, our dad actually seemed to have a genuine interest in Horatio and me. Sometimes, it felt worse knowing that he cared. It had been easier to ignore him. Now, I had to figure out my father all over again just as I was trying to figure out myself. I sighed heavily and let my fingers dance across the new leaves. I missed Mom. She would have loved Julie...and Rayne. And she would have been able to tell me what to do next.

As the thought crossed my mind, I heard a soft buzz of a bee and was surprised to see a small insect hovering just before me. I suppressed every instinct I had to swat it away. After all, if it belonged to Rayne, it was just out hunting pollen. Of course, if Rayne was playing with

Cassidy and me, there was no bee in the world big enough to quell my fury.

"Go tell Rayne he better not be sleeping with Cassidy or I'm going to kill him," I told the bee who dodged from side to side then set off.

I laughed, shaking my head, then followed the sound of Dad's and Horatio's voices. They were standing at the edge of the vineyard surveying an empty field. Horatio was still dressed in a business suit, but Dad was wearing jeans. It was unusual to see my dad dressed so casually. It looked...awkward.

"Plotting world domination?" I called.

Horatio turned and smiled at me, but he had an odd expression on his face. He looked...nervous? Okay, seriously, what was going on?

"No, plotting sparkling wine," my father answered.

The enologist in me immediately got to thinking, considering which grapes and what processes would work best. For years I'd tried to convince my dad to brew a sparkling wine. And now, just when I wanted to leap into a new trade, he was finally considering it. "Well, that is news."

"I thought you'd be pleased," Dad said with a smile. "Your mother always liked this view," he said, looking across the field toward the lake. "Roger has been monitoring this section of the vineyard for the last two seasons.

He says the climate will sustain the grapes we need. Maybe you can talk to him, Viola?"

"Sure," I said. "I'd love to. I have a whole notebook full of ideas somewhere."

My dad smiled. "Thought so. And, now that you're here, maybe Horatio will finally spit out whatever he's been trying to tell me for the last half an hour."

I laughed. "You do look pale," I told my brother who smiled at me. "Never could hide your emotions."

Horatio grinned. "Well, I have some good news, I think."

My dad bent to pick a dandelion which he then handed to me.

"Spit it out," I told Horatio as I stuck the little flower behind my ear.

"I...I was in Sweet Water this morning, met with Julie's dad. I'm going to ask Julie to marry me at the ball tomorrow."

My tears started welling at once. My big brother had found his love. I was so happy for him. I wrapped my arms around him and hugged him tight. "Congrats! Please tell me you got her a good ring."

"Well, duh," he said as I pulled back. "I just wanted to make sure, you know, that it was going to be okay?" he said then, looking at Dad.

My father and Julie had gotten off to a bad start.

Dad had wanted the property that later became Julie's shop. The tug-of-war between them had almost killed the spark between Horatio and Julie. But in the end, it was that same tension that had given Horatio the strength to stand up to Dad. And to this day, I wasn't quite sure what Julie had done to soften my father, but I knew something she'd said, or done, had won him over.

Dad smiled. "Horatio, you and Julie were meant for one another. Of course you have my blessing."

Horatio grinned. "Wait until you see what I have planned."

"I'm sure it will be epic," I said with a wink. "Congrats."

"Indeed, congratulations," Dad added.

"Well, she hasn't said yes yet."

"She will," I said with a smile. "I also have news. Nothing that fabulous, but it's an opportunity I want to take. I was offered an internship."

"At the college?" Dad asked.

I shook my head. "In France, at the Beaumont perfumery."

My brother, who knew my true goals, nodded. "Do it. It's just what you've been dreaming of."

"So you'd be gone the whole summer?" Dad asked.

"Maybe. I know you need me here. I wasn't sure

about the timing, but Luc Beaumont offered, and it's a great opportunity."

"Is this what you want?" Dad asked.

"Yes. I want to get some hands-on experience then come back and set up shop in the old distillery, start my own perfume label. I've even been considering opening a day spa."

My dad nodded. "Cottage industry. That could work very well."

I grinned. "Yes, it could. And I have a good nose for it. Of course, I'm going to need some acres for flowers. But not here. Make a sparkling wine here."

"We'll put you in the back along Rayne's property, let his bees work for you," Dad said.

At the mention of Rayne's name, my cheeks started burning. Unable to hide it, I noticed Horatio look closely at me then furrow his brow, looking perplexed.

"Well, how about that," my dad said then, sitting. He propped his elbows on his knees and gazed out at the lake. "Big news. Good news. Proud of you both," he said. There was a wistful acceptance in his voice that would not have been there in months past. And, I dare say, the sound of pride.

Horatio sighed. "And now, I should probably head back."

I looked at my phone. No return call from Rayne yet,

and I needed to get ready for my shift at Falling Waters. "Me too. Coming, Dad?"

"No. I think I'll sit here a bit," he replied, looking out over the field.

I leaned in, setting a light kiss on the top of his head. He grabbed my hand, patting it gently, then let me go.

With that, Horatio and I turned and headed back toward the parking lot.

"Cool about the internship, but you've got something else on your mind," Horatio said. "Spit it out."

"I don't know. You're going to be mad. Actually, right now, I might be mad. I'm confused. If I tell you, you won't do or say anything unless I say so. Promise me."

"Uh, no. I can't promise that."

"Then I'm not telling you anything."

"Yes, you are. Tell me. No, don't tell me. I see it on your face. A guy. Wait, not that Luc guy, right? I thought Alice—"

"No, not Luc."

"So it is a guy thing?"

"Do you know Rayne's friend, Cassidy?"

"Cassidy? Wait, are you hot for Cassidy? I didn't think you—"

"Oh my god, shut up. She's pretty enough, but no. Are Cassidy and Rayne an item?"

At that, Horatio stopped in his tracks. "Why do you care?"

"Just. Well. Are they or aren't they?"

"You didn't answer my question."

"You didn't answer *my* question."

"I think they're just friends. I never saw anything between then. Now, tell me why. Rayne...did Rayne make a move on you?"

"It's not like that. I have feelings for Rayne."

"For Rayne?"

"Yes."

"Rayne?"

"Yes. Shut up. So, well, am I stupid or what?"

Horatio was scowling. "Viola, are you sure? You two are so different from each other."

"Opposites attract."

"Have you talked to him about it? I mean, is it a thing?"

"We kissed."

"You kissed? When?"

"At Julie's."

"I think I may kill someone," Horatio said, looking pale once more.

I laughed. "No. Don't. Well, not yet. I need to see what Rayne's up to first. I mean, if he's genuine, I want to be with him. So don't mess things up."

"You and Rayne?"

"Yes."

"You? And Rayne?"

"Yes. That's what I've been saying."

"I'll go talk to him."

"No. Listen, you worry about Julie right now. I'll sort out this business with Rayne, and if you need to kill him, I'll let you know. We can hide the body together."

Horatio laughed then put his arm around me. "I will say this, Rayne is a loyal friend. He's amazingly kind and generous. He's not rich, but he's a happy person. If you do care for him, and he does care for you, the two of you could get along fabulously. And if not, I know a great place to dig."

I laughed then pulled out my phone once more. When I did, I saw I'd missed a call from Rayne. Ugh! Cell service was always spotty in the vineyard.

"That's a start," I said, showing Horatio my phone. "You're sure about Cassidy?"

"Yeah, he told me once he understands our relationship because Cassidy is like a sister to him. It's not a thing."

I exhaled deeply.

"He's taking you to the ball tomorrow night, right?"

I nodded.

"Well, you'll see for sure then. And so will I. I'll have my eye on him."

It was then that I stopped cold, grabbing Horatio's arm. "Oh shit!"

"What?"

"I forgot to buy a dress!" Wonderful. In the middle of all the excitement going on around me, I'd somehow forgotten to buy myself a gown. How in the world had that happened? I'd prodded Alice along to get hers, but somehow it had just slipped off my radar. With the symposium, and Beaumont, and Rayne, I'd totally forgotten.

"Stumble into that closet of yours. I bet you have something in there you forgot you even own."

"Very funny," I said with a frown, but then my mind was struck with an idea. "I'll come up with something."

I opened my car door.

"Don't forget to take those boots off," Horatio reminded me.

"Crap. My head is a mess," I said. Pulling off the boots, I handed them to my brother who tossed them in the trunk.

"Muddy boots and designer pants. I don't know, seems like you and Rayne might work after all," Horatio said with a grin as he leaned against my car.

I smiled at my brother. "Shut up. Anyway, I'm so excited for you. I love Julie."

"Me too. Tomorrow at midnight."

"I'll be there," I said then started the ignition.

Horatio stepped away from the car and waved good-bye.

I smiled. If only Mom could see us now.

CHAPTER 13

rayne

After I left the suit shop, I walked down to the lakeshore. I'd tried to call Viola back, but she didn't pick up. I knew Cassidy meant no harm, but I'd sensed Viola's suspicion the night we'd gone to Falling Waters. Like all faerie, Cassidy had a sparkly glow. No doubt Viola had noticed it, and it had set her on edge. Certainly Cassidy had gotten Rick's attention, when he wasn't too busy casting glances at Viola.

I looked at my phone once more. It was almost time for her to start work at the restaurant. Now what?

I walked slowly down the beach eyeing the dark blue waters as they lapped against the rocky shoreline. The sun was starting to set, trimming the sky with deep purple and vibrant pink colors. The water reflected its shimmering light, each crest trimmed with the vibrant hues.

I closed my eyes and felt the soft wind blowing off the lake. The sweet perfume of spring filled my nose. I was not surprised when, a moment later, I heard a familiar buzzing sound. Two of my little ones had found me.

Opening my eyes, I listened as they reported in. Alice was happily preparing for her dinner tonight, and Luc was over at Lavender Fields Bed and Breakfast trying to figure out what to wear. And both of them were delightfully happy. The bees, magical creatures that they are, did what they could to help plant romantic ideas in both their minds. Everything, it seemed, was finally coming along for Alice. But long distance relationships rarely worked well. Did that mean that in order to help my girl, I was going to have to lose her?

"Well done," I whispered to my friends who then directed my attention toward a figure walking down the beach toward me.

I cast a glance down the beach to see Kate, with whom Alice would be having dinner that evening, walking along the lakeshore.

"Rayne," she called happily.

Her long golden hair was blowing in the soft wind. She was a lovely thing.

"Hi, Kate," I said, stuffing my hands in my pockets, walking to meet her.

"I'm not sure if I should be happy with you and Viola Hunter or angry. Alice is head over heels for this Frenchmen you introduced her to. If she runs off to France, I may never speak to you again."

I laughed. "Let's go with happy. You're having them over tonight?"

"Yeah, Cooper and I wanted to check this guy out."

"He seems a good sort."

Kate nodded, her bright eyes shining. She looked closely at me then said, "Something's troubling you."

"How did you know?"

"You're here," she said, motioning toward the water.

I smiled at her. Alice and Kate had been friends for many years. Alice's report of her was always good, and moreover, Alice trusted her. That was good enough for me. "In love, I think. Not sure if she loves me back."

"Hmm," Kate mused. "I know how you can find out."

I raised an eyebrow at her.

"Ask," she replied playfully, giggling. The sound of her laughter, I noticed then, chimed like a bell which echoed on the waves. The sound of it was captivating. For a moment, I felt transfixed. Strange.

Kate took my arm, seemingly breaking the spell, then turned and walked with me down the beach. "Love is something so rare, and never easy to come by, not true love, at least. If you love this woman, tell her. What's the risk? I once had to make a great leap of faith for love. It wasn't an easy choice, but I did whatever it took."

"Did you get what you wanted?"

"You've met my husband? Seen my children? Their worth is beyond measure. And the cost, well," she said, glancing across the waves, "seems very small in comparison now. If you love her, truly love her, do anything for her. Do everything you can to make sure she knows what she means to you."

Kate's words struck my heart. It was exactly what I needed to hear. "Thank you, Kate."

"Of course," she said then took my hand. Opening it, she lay two pieces of beach glass in my palm. I noticed then how the tiny pieces, one pale pink in color, the other one green, looked like hearts. "I was wondering who they were for. Now I know," she said, then closed my hand.

The sun dropped below the clouds and dipped toward the horizon. It cast stunning pink and golden light on the beach. In that moment, the air around Kate shifted and changed. What a sparkly thing she was, all golden and glimmering in the sunlight. She was luminescent. And there seemed to be no other place in the world where she fit more perfectly than on that beach. And in that moment, I knew without a doubt what I had long guessed.

"Mermaid?" I inquired softly.

Kate giggled lightly, her voice like a small melodious bell. "Once. No more. And you, fey thing that you are...I remember another like you in Chancellor many years ago. No wings though, huh?"

"Those are pixies."

"Thought I saw one in my garden last summer. Wasn't sure if that was you or not. I thought maybe you could shrink down and ride in a walnut."

"I wish."

Kate squeezed my hand then let me go. "I need to get back, finish getting ready for dinner tonight. Good luck, Rayne."

"Thank you."

"Not going to forgive you though if she moves to France, though."

"Won't shipwreck me, will you?"

"Retired," she said with a laugh then headed back down the beach.

I watched her as she went. A lovely creature, she melded into the beachline. Mermaid. Chancellor really was a special place. With all the witches haunting the ladies' auxiliary and beauty salons, of course it made sense that we'd have our own mermaid.

I smiled. If the bees and I could finally find a match for Alice, there was no way I could mess things up with Viola. I just needed to show her that she was, beyond all measure, the thing I wanted most in the world. And I was willing to do anything to have her...even ask her brother's permission.

CHAPTER 14

viola

"Maybe this trunk, Miss Hunter?" Dorothea asked, pulling an old box out of the back of my mother's closet.

I was standing on the other side of the room looking in the garment bags hanging at the back of Dad's closet. So far I'd found a few gowns, but not the one I was looking for.

Dorothea opened the trunk to reveal a dress box inside.

"Oh my gosh, that's it!" I squealed.

I don't know why the idea came to me, but the second Horatio told me to go check in my closets for a dress, I remembered an amazing blue gown my mother had once worn to some formal event. I remembered, very vividly, her coming down the stairs in the midnight blue gown which was covered in glimmering beads and intricately sewn embroidery. Stars and moons had been sewn with sparkling beading all along the sheer material covering the skirt of the vintage dress. She'd sparkled like the night's sky. It was an image of my mother I always carried in my heart.

"I can't believe you found it," I said, gently lifting the dress out of the box.

Carefully, Dorothea and I looked over the garment.

"It will need a few stitches. You're a bit smaller than your mother was. I can have it ready for you by tomorrow. Let's try it on," she said as I quickly slipped off my clothes and slid into the gown.

It was large, and the material was very fragile, but something magical happened when that dress slipped over my head. A dizzy feeling took over me, and I swore I could hear music. The feel of Rayne's lips pressed against mine, and his sweet honey taste came to mind. I closed my eyes, feeling myself swoon.

"You all right, Miss Hunter?"

"Yes. Hungry, I think. I've been running all day."

"All day? All year, more like."

She was definitely right about that. And now, I'd be running even more. I needed to connect with Luc, let him know I was unquestionably interested in the apprenticeship. And I needed a spare moment to return Rayne's call.

I just wanted to make sure I was in the right frame of mind when I did so. I hadn't had a chance to get there yet.

"Look how beautiful," Dorothea said, standing me in front of the mirror.

The vintage dress was as stunning as ever. One of the sleeves had ripped a bit and the satin sash needed to be fixed, but the hem was the right length. It was so lovely. And more than that, I caught the light scent of my mother's perfume on the fabric. Was there anything more perfect than feeling her in that moment?

Carefully, Dorothea eyed the waist. "About two inches will do. I'll just fold it in, don't want to cut the actual gown. No need to hem. You and your mother must have been the same height."

"Yes," I replied, staring at myself in the mirror. How happy my mother had looked the night she wore this gown. I didn't even know where she'd gone. I suddenly missed her terribly.

"You have a date for the ball?" Dorothea asked as she helped me out of the gown.

"Yes. I'm going with Rayne."

Dorothea chuckled. "Better make sure he has a tux."

"Already checked," I replied, joining her laughter.

"I like that boy, though. He turns the ladies' heads, but he doesn't seem to have his mind on anyone. He's just busy out in his fields. Are you going as friends or..."

"As more than friends…a new development."

"Well, how about that? And here I always imagined you with some CEO, not a beekeeper. It's a good choice, Viola. That kind of man will always stay by your side."

"You think?"

She smiled at me. "Yes."

My cell chimed. I was late. "Crap."

"Good thing you're the boss, Miss Hunter."

"You're right about that," I said then looked at the dress. "You sure it will be okay?"

"Oh, we'll get it ready in time. Not a thing to worry about. Now you just need to find a pair of shoes."

Shoes. Dammit. Well, that was a problem for tomorrow. And a good problem to have. I was never sad to have a reason to look for a new pair of shoes.

I ARRIVED AT THE RESTAURANT HALF AN HOUR later to find the place completely packed. There were at least two dozen people outside waiting for a table. And, of course, problems abounded. The outside heat lamps weren't working, the lamb chops delivered that morning —for the evening's special—had gone bad, and two waitresses were out with the flu. While I'd agreed to take over the management of the restaurant for the first year, nothing could have been further from my real intentions and desires.

Taking a deep breath, I dove in and spent the night racing from problem to problem. As I waited tables, made salads, ran the register, and called repairmen, it seemed like the world was working in chorus to remind me just how far being a restaurateur was from my real dream.

Pausing just a moment at the bar to take a break, I pulled out my phone to see I'd missed calls from Horatio, Alice, and two calls from Rayne.

Crap.

I was never going to get a chance to call him. My feet hurt, I was sweating, and I was totally exhausted, but it no longer mattered. I didn't want him second guessing. I'd grab a quick drink then give him a call.

I slipped behind the bar a moment to pour myself a glass of water when I heard a familiar laugh coming from the other end of the bar. Much to my surprise, I spotted a familiar redhead sitting there. Cassidy. She was eating a huge basket of calamari while Rick was slinging mixed drinks like a madman, all the while flirting with the girl.

Now, what in the hell was she doing here? Why did I keep running into this girl?

"Cassidy?" I called, heading down to the end of the bar.

"Miss Hunter?" one of the chefs called from the kitchen.

"One sec," I replied.

"Hey, Vi," Cassidy said, grinning at me. "Awesome calamari."

"Thanks. I'm surprised to see you."

"Yeah, long day. I wanted something tasty to reward myself," she said. "And I'm trying to convince Rick to come to my hot yoga class."

Rick laughed as he dropped cherries into the drinks he was making.

"Well, did she convince you?" I asked him.

"Apparently I'm going to sweat my ass off first thing tomorrow morning."

I grinned. "I'm sure you can handle it."

Rick shook his head, laughing, then lifted a tray of drinks. "We'll see. Excuse me a sec," he said then took the drinks to one of the servers.

"I sure as hell hope he doesn't sweat that sweet ass off. The food here is awesome, but the view is even better," Cassidy said, lifting her drink and taking a sip. "Fixation worthy, even."

"Rick is single, but I thought maybe you and Rayne…"

"Miss Hunter?" one of the chefs called again.

"Just one minute," I replied.

Cassidy burst out laughing. "Rayne? No way. He's like a brother to me. Besides, he's got his eyes...elsewhere," she said, winking at me. "Oh! Speaking of, did he call you back?" she asked, popping another bite.

I was an idiot. My worries about Rayne and Cassidy were completely pointless. I was stupid to think Rayne would play me. He wasn't like that. I suddenly felt very childish.

"Yeah, um, he tried," I said, pulling out my phone. "I've been swamped all day. We can't reach one another. I was just going to call him back."

"He was trying on tuxes when you called this morning. I went with him, tried to save you some embarrassment."

"You were at the suit shop?"

She nodded then lifted the olive out her drink. "Yeah. I think he was afraid he was going to mess up and look stupid. You know his wardrobe basically consists of jeans and flannel shirts. He wanted some advice. I think he only called me because he was too nervous to ask your brother. Well, anyway... Um, I think that guy is bleeding," she said then, pointing behind me.

I turned around to see Charles, the sous chef, trying

to discreetly hold a heavy towel around his hand. The fabric was turning red, and the chef was turning white.

Oh shit. "Charles? What happened?"

"Knife slipped. I need to go to the ER."

"Oh god. I'm so sorry. We'll get Kenny to drive," I said, referring to one of the bus boys. "I'll call Erica in to work."

"You sure? The place is nuts."

"You're bleeding," I said, aghast. "Of course I'm sure. I insist."

He nodded then headed into the back.

"Sorry, I need to go," I told Cassidy. "Nice to see you again. And thanks for your help with the suit," I said with a grin, suddenly feeling a bit guilty for forcing Rayne so far out of his element just to please me. Maybe I was doing the wrong thing. "Oh, and enjoy the yoga tomorrow."

Cassidy winked at me, tipping her drink in toast.

I hurried back to the kitchen. Kenny had already grabbed his keys, and he and Charles were headed out the back door.

"Call me as soon as you get there," I told Kenny. "Let me know what happens. We'll take care of everything, you just get patched up," I told Charles.

He nodded and they headed out.

I went into the office just off the kitchen to phone

Erica, our other sous chef. As I walked, I sent Rayne a quick text:

Sorry I keep missing you. Slammed today. Restaurant is so busy. Everything okay?

Perfect. See you tomorrow night at six?

Yes, please. Pick me up?

Need to get my pumpkin and mice in order first.

Naturally. Thank you, again, for agreeing to take me.

Anything for you.

I set the phone down and stared at the last message. My emotions tripped over themselves, each begging to be heard first. This was either the beginning of a great love affair or a great heartache. I wasn't sure which. But more than anything, I couldn't wait to find out.

rayne

The following morning, I wandered into the massive ballroom at Arden Estate, which sat along the shoreline of Lake Erie, looking for Horatio. The estate, a gem which now belonged to the Chancellor Historical Society, had once been the home to Archibald Arden, captain of the shipping industry in Lake Erie. While Chancellor's trade had turned from its roots to wine and education, the first money man in Chancellor had been a sailor and captain of commerce. The touches of old money were everywhere. The Historical Society had lovingly restored the old building, with the help of the city, the Chancellor Arts Council, Chancellor College, and Blushing Grape Vineyards, but the annual Cherry Blossom Ball kept the old estate flush with cash for day to day expenses. The Cherry Blossom Ball was so-named in part for the cherry trees on the property, all of which were currently blooming with pearly white and pink blossoms. The event also celebrated Chancellor's relationship with its Japanese sister city. Cherry blossom viewing, an important rite of spring in Japan, provided the perfect venue for the ball. And my friend, Horatio Hunter, was responsible for making the event come off without a hitch.

"Thank you, Jennifer. Yes, over there," I heard Horatio say, directing a florist with a cart full of flowers toward the other side of the room. Completely lost in his work, his finger gliding across the screen of his tablet, he hadn't noticed me enter.

I cast a glance around the room. The orchestra was all set up, and some of the musicians were there testing the acoustics. Violins and flutes filled the massive old room with the soft sounds of a waltz. Nicely bedecked tables, still being dressed by the florist's team, circled the marble ballroom floor. I cast a glance up at the stained glass windows. Each window featured Chancellor images: the waterwheel outside Falling Waters restaurant, the Grove, a public park noted for its ties to the witches said to have once lived in Chancellor—and of course they still did live there, you just had to know where to look—and a blonde-haired mermaid with a glimmering blue-green tail.

I inhaled and exhaled deeply once more. Horatio and

I had been friends for years. Before Julie came onto the scene, and before I'd started seeing Viola for who she really was, Horatio and I had our fun. What would he think now that I'd turned my attention to his sister?

Mustering up my courage, I approached him. "Got the canapes in order?" I called cheerfully.

Horatio stopped working and looked up at me. He smiled, but a weird expression crossed his face. Tonight was the night. There was no doubt that Julie would agree to marry him, but surely he was nervous. I knew I would be.

"Man," he said, "you have no idea. Everything with the event is in order, thank god. Oysters went bad but otherwise, all good. Honestly, I couldn't be less worried about the actual event. It's the rest. I should have just taken Julie to the beach and asked her in private. Instead, well, I wanted her to know her value. Midnight. Don't get too far in case I pass out."

"No worries. I'll be here."

"With my sister," he replied, and this time I heard the hard edge on his voice.

"Yeah, about that...You and I have been friends for years. You know I've never been serious about anyone before—"

"What about Cassidy?" Horatio asked, interrupting.

I would have laughed out loud if it weren't for the

look on Horatio's face. "Cassidy? No, she's just..." *Another faerie, like me,* I wanted to say. "A family friend."

"You sure?"

It was clear to me then that Horatio and Viola had talked. I wasn't sure what had been said, but clearly Cassidy was cause for concern. If they only knew the truth...well, that truth would come later. "Positive. My brother," I said then, clapping his shoulder. "Look, I need to be straight with you. My feelings for Viola...changed. I want to take things with her to another level. I'm serious about her, and I think she feels something for me too. I'm done with playing. I respect you, and I don't want anything to be weird between us, but I really care for Viola."

Horatio studied my face closely, smiled, then said, "The women of Chancellor will be crushed if you take your twinkle off the market."

I shrugged, feeling a massive weight melt off my shoulders. "Doesn't matter. No one ever had a twinkle for me...until Viola. That's something I can't let go."

Horatio nodded. "Do right by her."

"I will. And in the meantime, what can I do for you?"

Horatio shook his head. "Just wish me luck."

"None needed. Julie loves you."

Horatio smiled. "What happened to us?"

"Amazing women. Time for something new, something better," I said then looked around the room once more. This time, I noticed that one of the stained glass windows depicted a woman in a flowing gown and a small twig in her hand. The glass around her was cut to shimmer with opalescent light. A faerie?

"Cheers to that," Horatio said, then with a sigh, he looked at his tablet once more.

"I should let you get back to work. Sure you don't need anything?"

"No. Thanks, though. See you tonight. You'll be late. Viola is never ready on time. Too many shoe options."

"I'd wait a century for her."

"Don't let her know that."

I grinned. "Don't be nervous. It's going to go great."

"Thanks. See you tonight," he said, then turned back to his work.

I walked back toward the front of the building but paused just a moment before I went outside. Pulling my willow wand from my back pocket, I twirled it once around my fingers then aimed it at Horatio:

With the heart of a lion
Let him delight
And fully embrace his magical night.

A glimmering golden light quickly moved from my wand across the hall and zipped around Horatio. He didn't seem to notice the light, but he did pause, and his posture changed. The spell had worked. Technically, we weren't supposed to use our faerie magic on anyone other than our assignments, but love magic was my business. What would one charm hurt? As the thought crossed my mind, my eyes were drawn once more to the stained glass image of the faerie on the window. And for a brief moment, I swore the image moved. I frowned and looked harder but nothing seemed amiss. It must have been a brief shift in the light, that was all.

I headed outside to find delivery trucks driving in and out of the impressive estate. I headed back to my truck, passing a water fountain depicting a lovely mermaid. Next time I met Ziggy and Skyla, I needed to ask about the former owner of the property. Whomever he was, he clearly was tuned into the mythology of Chancellor. Like all great stories, there was truth buried behind the fairy tale.

viola

"Oh my god oh my god oh my god," Alice said, pacing her living room apartment above her bagel shop. "This is like something from a fairy tale. How can this be happening?"

It was the morning of the Cherry Blossom Ball, and Alice, who'd woken me with panic texts, was a hot mess. "Calm your tits down, girl," I said with a laugh as I finished polishing my toe nails. Setting the paint aside for a moment, I sipped the mimosa Alice had made for me.

"Okay, I'll calm one tit down...but not my party tit," she said, making us both giggle. "This never happens to me. He's hot. He's rich. He's French. And he seems to legit like me. We've been staying up all night just talking. He gets me. And I get him. He's staying an extra week. Says he can't go back yet."

"Just go with the flow. If it's working, let it work," I said then gazed out the window. *Take your own advice, Viola.*

"Speaking of," Alice said, seeming to read my mind, "What is going on with you and Rayne?" She flopped down in a chair and grabbed her drink, polishing off half the champagne flute.

"Going on?" I asked innocently, turning my attention back to my sparkly blue toes as I touched up the paint.

Alice laughed. "At Julie's barbeque....there was a vibe there. I mean, there's always been a vibe between you too, but it was amped. And then there is the ball tonight."

"Well..." I said then looked up at Alice who was looking at me expectantly.

"Well?"

I grinned. "I don't know. I'm just seeing him differently these days. He's all wrong for me, but I guess I just... I want him."

"No. Way," Alice said then jumped up. "I knew it! That boy's eyes are as big as moons every time he looks at you. So what are you going to do?"

"Go slow. Did Luc tell you about the apprenticeship he offered me?"

Alice nodded. "Mentioned it."

"It's time to get my life back on track. I have so many dreams. My own perfume line. A day spa here in Chancellor. More ideas than I can manage to keep a lid on. I want to go to France this summer. Dad said it was okay. But for me and Rayne, it's bad timing. I can't ask him to wait around for me."

"If he can't wait one summer, he isn't worth waiting for...even if he is my friend. Just tell him. It won't be a big deal."

I nodded, hoping she was right. "We'll sort it out."

"Oh man, this is going to be an awesome night. So, Horatio told me...tonight at midnight he's going to ask Julie to marry him. Oh my god, I can't wait. Julie's going to be your sister."

I lifted my champagne flute. "To finding a love like Julie's and Horatio's?"

"I'll drink to that. Cheers," Alice said, clicking her glass against mine.

Sipping the sweet drink, I thought once more about Rayne. Tonight, we'd either go for it or decide the timing wasn't right. I hoped Rayne would be willing to wait. Hell, if Cinderella could win a prince at a ball, why couldn't I land a hippie beekeeper?

"Miss Hunter?" Dorothea called. "It's almost seven."

"Shoes!" I called helplessly. "I swear to god, I'm so scattered. I never even looked," I opened box after box of shoes, but nothing seemed quite right. My hair, which had been pulled up in a perfect loose bun, was suddenly starting to slump. If I started sweating, that would be the end of my makeup.

"Rhinestones? The ones you wore a couple of years back to the Dickens event?"

"I forgot about those. The buckle was a little loose though," I said, scanning the boxes for the shoes she mentioned.

"I'll go grab the pliers. We'll squeeze them shut. Go get dressed. Your date is downstairs waiting."

Finally eyeing the box, I pulled it from the shelf. The lid slipped off as the box jarred sideways. I managed to catch the shoes as the box tumbled to the floor. A tiny slip of paper fluttered out.

Clutching the shoes, I grabbed the paper only to discover my mother's handwriting thereon. It startled me. While our home was full of her touches, there was something so personal about finding a note written in her hand.

"For my beautiful daughter. Spotted these at a shop

downtown. Knew they were for you. Looking forward to our special time tonight."

My mind reeled back in time, remembering how Mom and I had attended a Christmas event at the college which included a showing of *A Christmas Carol*. It wasn't long after that she'd gotten sick. Before we knew it, she was gone.

I closed my eyes and clutched the shoes against my chest.

"Miss you, Mom," I whispered. I inhaled deeply then rose. Setting the shoes aside, I slipped on the blue gown. It fit me like a glove.

"Oh, Miss Hunter!" Dorothea said, entering the room once more. "You look beautiful! How does it fit?"

"Perfect," I said, checking the sleeve Dorothea had repaired. "You've done a wonderful job."

"Just watch this seam in the back," she said as she turned to zip me up. "I've never seen stitches like these before. Stubborn. Almost like the dress had a mind of its own," she said with a laugh. "But, with a little coaxing, she cooperated. There you go," she said then, turning me toward the mirror.

The image looking at me was an echo of my mother. The sparkles on the blue fabric glimmered like stars. The intricate silver threading in the embroidery shimmered.

The fabric on the skirt was light and soft, the bodice decorated intricately.

"Rayne is downstairs," Dorothea said then. "Shall we get these shoes on?"

I nodded. Carefully gathering the skirt, I sat on the bed while Dorothea slipped the shoes on.

"I'm back to your senior prom," Dorothea said with a laugh.

"Don't remind me. You remember when Conner got out of the limo, how his pant leg lifted up to reveal his white socks? I thought Dad was going to pass out."

Dorothea laughed. "I'm not sure who was more shocked, him or Conner, especially when Mr. Hunter went inside only to come back with a pair of black socks."

I laughed. "Yeah, that was the end of that prospect."

"Well, the prospect downstairs is looking rather dapper tonight, if I do say so myself."

"Does he now?"

"Honey, I'm old, not dead."

We both laughed out loud.

"Okay, let me just squeeze the clasp," she said, applying the pliers. "There. Now, you're going to have a time getting them off, but they should stay put."

"Thank you, Dorothea."

"Anything, my dear. Wish your mama was here

tonight. Mr. Hunter told me Horatio is planning to propose to Miss Dayton."

I nodded. "Big night."

"Well, you enjoy yourself too," she said, holding out her hand to help me up.

Taking one last glance into the mirror, I adjusted a curl behind my ear, grabbed my clutch purse, and headed downstairs. The sparkling shoes wobbled for just a moment as I slid into them.

Heels, fail me not.

rayne

I nervously toyed with the crystal figurines sitting on a table as I waited for Viola. The moment I realized, however, that the little ornaments would probably cost me a month's income, I stuck my hand in my pocket and went to look out the sliding glass doors leading to the gardens outside. It was already dark. The garden fountains were illuminated with soft light.

"Rayne?" Viola called.

The sound of her voice swept across the room and gripped my faerie heart more strongly than any spell ever had. I turned to see her coming carefully down the stairs, a vision of beauty, like she was wearing the starry sky wrapped around her. More than her gown or anything else, however, it was the look in her eyes that moved me most. There was a glimmer in there I'd never seen before.

For the first time, I felt what it was like to be victim to someone else's sparkle.

She crossed the room and took my hand. After a moment, she laughed. "Well, say something."

"I...I...stunning."

She smiled softly. "I suppose that will do. And you," she said then, gently stroking the lapel of my suit, "you clean up nicely."

"Don't tell me you were really expecting flannel and jeans?" I joked.

She smiled once more, the look on her face illuminating the entire room. "Of course not. But I understand you had some help. Looks like I'll have to thank Cassidy."

"Wait, I saved the best part," I said. "In the truck, though. You ready?"

Viola nodded. "Night, Dorothea," she called to the housekeeper who was standing on the upstairs landing, dabbing her eyes with a hankie.

Taking Viola's hand in mine, I led her outside. The air was warm for a spring night in Chancellor. The smell of flowers wafted off the garden. In the distance, I could hear the call of frogs. There was magic in the air. I could feel it all around me. If I hadn't known better, I would have suspected some faerie magic at work. Grinning, I opened the passenger door, leaned inside, and grabbed my top hat and cane, popping the top hat on.

"Madame, your coach," I said with a bow.

Viola laughed. "How gentlemanly of you, Mr. Darcy," she replied with a polite nod then got in.

I went around to the other side, slid in, and clicked the engine on. To my great relief, the truck started, and we headed off. I turned the old radio to a classical music station and drove toward Arden Estate. I tried to pretend my nerves weren't bothering me, but they were. The event tonight would change all our lives: Julie's and Horatio's, Alice's, and, I hoped, mine. I hadn't felt this awkward in ages. My twinkle always saved me. Along with a few silver-tongued lines and my looks, I never worried about how I'd score with the ladies. But around Viola, I was a mess. I always fancied myself an Oberon, but tonight, I was operating a lot more like Tinker Bell's awkward second cousin.

Viola's phone buzzed. "Alice," she said, flipping through the messages. "She and Luc are there. Julie and Horatio. Told her we're on our way. Not that she'll have eyes for anyone but Luc anyway. God, it's like love at first sight. I thought that only happened in movies," Viola said wistfully.

Reaching across the seat, I took her hand, lacing her fingers in mine. "Well, that's not the only way to fall in love."

Viola squeezed my hand in reply. "Rayne," she whispered softly. My name had never sounded more beautiful. "Lovely night," she whispered, gazing out the window.

"Lovely woman," I replied.

"Oh, shut up," she said teased.

"I mean it."

She was silent for a minute then laughed.

"What is it?"

"Horatio is going to kill you."

I smirked. "No, he isn't."

"No?"

"No. I talked to him today."

"Wait, what? You like, got his blessing?"

I turned to look at her. She had the funniest expression on her face, at once she seemed both pleased and surprised. I lifted her hand and kissed it.

At that, Viola only laughed, but her laughter was joyous and happy, and it made my heart sing.

WE ARRIVED AT THE MAGNIFICENT ARDEN Estate just a short drive later. The entire place was lit up. Black limos and all manner of high end cars pulled into the front lot where valets stood waiting.

While my truck raised a few eyebrows, no one said a word. I handed the keys over to the valet and went to the passenger side to meet Viola.

"Jeez, glad I washed her," I said, shooting a glance back at my old pickup.

Viola laughed out loud. "All this," she said, waving her hand at the assembled crowd. "Is so...expected. Boring. You stand out," she said, then reached up and took me by the chin, giving it a little shake.

"I'm nothing compared to you, Miss Hunter. Shall we?" I asked, motioning to the entryway.

As we climbed the stairs, we were treated with the lovely sounds of the orchestra. The music rolled out of the massive building, filling the night with the dulcet tones of the waltz. All around us, gentlemen dressed in fine suits and ladies in beautiful gowns headed inside. It was like all of Chancellor's old money had come out for the event. Several people called to Viola. Putting on her best wine-heiress smile, she nodded and waved to them.

"No escaping it," she said quietly with a sigh. "Wherever I go, I'm Blushing Grape Vineyards."

"No," I said, stopping. Taking her gently by the waist, I turned her to look out over the cherry orchard that surrounded the estate. In the distance, the dark waves of Lake Erie glimmered in the moonlight. The pink and white cherry blossoms in the orchard, sitting between us and the shoreline, created a magnificent and a gentle canvas. The leaves, reflecting the silver moonlight, danced in the wind. The scent of the cherry blossoms perfumed the air. "You are so much more. All nature bends its eyes just to look at you. See," I said, and then very discreetly, pulled my little willow wand from my jacket pocket and gave it a wave. The wind blew once more, and this time, it caught the pearl-colored petals. With a soft, fragrant breeze, it marshalled them toward Viola. The wind blew the petals into a gentle torrent around us.

She laughed gently, reaching out to touch the petals, then turned toward me. "What was that?" she asked.

I shrugged. "You see, I was right."

Viola wrapped her arm around my waist, and we walked up the stairs. Mellow, golden-colored Japanese paper lanterns painted with images of cherry blossoms illuminated our steps. As we reached the top of the stair-case, Viola wobbled, then stopped. Pulling aside the skirt of her dress, she examined her shoe.

"Buckle," she said, then bent down to adjust it. "Dorothea tightened it, but I guess I better be careful."

"Can I help?"

She shook her head. "There, that will do for now," she said then reached out to me.

I steadied her as she rose. When she did so, however, a strange expression crossed her face.

"Oh my gosh, my dress. I think I felt something rip."

"Where?"

"The back, at the zipper."

Looking behind her, I examined the zipper alongside the intricate embroidery. Sure enough, it was ripped open.

"Is it torn?" she whispered, her voice shaking. "This was my mother's dress."

"Just a moment," I said, and moving deftly, my wand hidden in the sleeve of my coat, I gave it a wave. A tiny sparkle of light slipped up the back of the fabric, mending it. Gently, I checked the work. Perfect. "It's okay. One of the beads pulled out of place, must have given the fabric a tug. It's all right now."

"Thank goodness," she said then, looping her arm in mine. "I'd hate to think I ruined something that belonged to her. Okay, I think I'm ready. You?"

I smiled down at her, stroking her cheek with the back of my finger. "Beyond."

With that, the woman I was completely mad about and I entered the ball.

CHAPTER 18

viola

The scene inside the ballroom of Arden Estate was a feast for the senses. The room was full of Chancellor elites dressed in black tie and gowns of silk, jewels sparkling. Everywhere I looked, I saw pink and white cherry blossoms. Ornate arrangements illuminated by candlelight decorated the tables. There were stands of cherry blossom branches hung with paper lanterns all around the room. The room was alive with their pearly color and elements of twinkling gold. My nose was on fire with the smell of the beautiful, delicate flowers. I'd been to a few Cherry Blossom Balls, but by far, this was the most beautiful event I'd ever seen. Delegates from our Japanese sister city moved through the room sipping champagne as the orchestra played the dulcet tones of the *Edelweiss* waltz.

"Look," Rayne said, motioning to a couple on the dance floor.

Alice and Luc moved gracefully around the room, lost in one another's eyes. Alice's blue dress seemed to float around her as they drifted around the center of the ballroom dance floor under the glimmering lights of the crystal chandelier overhead.

"She looks so beautiful," I whispered. "I'm so happy for her."

Rayne was smiling as he looked on. "Me too. Ah, there's Julie and Horatio."

My brother stood smiling with his arm around his girlfriend's waist. They were near a craft table where, it seemed, Julie had prepared a cornucopia of cherry blossom inspired delights.

Rayne and I moved toward them.

"Not bad. Needs more tissue paper carnations and crepe paper though," I told Horatio.

"Yeah, and the balloon animal clown is late. Event ruined," he replied, then laughed.

"Viola, you look so beautiful," Julie said, letting go of my brother to come hug me.

I hugged her tightly, knowing she had no idea what the night had in store for her. I had to choke back my tears.

"You too," I said, pulling back to admire the pink,

blue, and white kimono she was wearing. She'd pulled her red dreadlocks up into a neat pile on her head and adorned her hair with cherry blossoms.

"Thanks! I wanted to fit in and lucked across this."

"Wow, Julie. Did you make all these?" Rayne asked, looking over the desserts.

At the center of the table was a tall cake made to look like a Japanese temple piped with cherry blossoms. On the table were tiered trays of cupcakes topped with crystalized blossoms, fondant blossoms, chocolate blossoms, and everything in between. She also had laid out delicate pink and white petit-fours topped with cherry blossoms and cookies shaped like the flowers.

"Totally inspired. Some are infused with the flower, some with cherry," she said, pointing. "And the other ingredients are, of course, secret," she added, winking at Rayne.

The gesture puzzled me, but I chalked it up to Julie's playfulness. I knew she only had eyes for my brother.

"I know that dress," Horatio said then, smiling at me. "I have to admit, my little sister looks beautiful. Good thing I know her date has manners."

Rayne bowed toward him.

"Viola? Rayne?" a soft voice called from behind us.

We turned to find Genevieve Harper, the owner of Lavender Fields Bed and Breakfast. She shifted nervously then smiled. She was wearing a lovely dress befitting the name of her business, the soft, violet-colored material trimmed with shining beads.

"Genevieve. So good to see you. I wasn't sure—" I began.

"Luc talked me into it," she explained then turned to Horatio. "It's a beautiful event, Mr. Hunter."

"Mr. Hunter is my father. Genevieve, right? I'm Horatio," he said, sticking out his hand. "I think we've seen one another at chamber meetings?"

She nodded. "Nice to meet you, Horatio."

"I'm Julie," Julie said, shaking the woman's hand.

"Did someone mention me?" my father asked as he joined us. Like the rest of the assembled men, he was dressed nicely in a tuxedo, a grape leaf on his lapel.

"Not too shabby," I told him, dusting off his shoulder.

He leaned in and kissed my cheek. "Your mom would love to see you in this, Viola," he said, admiring my gown then turned to Julie. He grinned at her flair, shook his head, then leaned in and kissed her cheek. "Adorable," he told her. "Now, what have you made today?" he asked, looking over her table.

"Try this," she told him, handing him a bite-sized petit-four.

My dad popped the confection. "Perfect," he said

between chews.

Julie giggled. "Glad you like it. Mission accomplished."

Rayne, I noticed, was grinning at Julie. I suddenly felt like I'd been left out on a joke.

"Mr. Hunter, have you met Genevieve Harper?" Rayne asked.

Dad turned and, I realized, noticed Genevieve for the first time. A strange expression crossed his face.

"N...no. Hello," he said, reaching out for her hand. "Aaron Hunter."

"Genevieve Harper," she replied.

"*Miss* Harper owns Lavender Fields Bed and Breakfast," I added quickly. I had never, ever, seen my dad look at anyone like that...well, not since my mom. It so surprised me that I found myself grinning. "She lodges most of Blushing Grape's out-of-town guests."

"Do you? Then I guess I owe you a thanks."

Genevieve smiled shyly. "My pleasure, Mr. Hunter."

"You're missing a drink, Miss Harper. I heard the champagne is flavored with cherry blossoms tonight. Might I get you one?" Dad said, extending his arm to her.

Genevieve blushed.

I shot a look at my brother. We exchanged a *"what the hell"* expression then tried not to stare. I couldn't believe my eyes. Was Dad making a move?

"Okay," Genevieve replied with an awkward smile then linked her arm in his.

With that, Dad left with the owner of the bed and breakfast, leaving me gawking in his wake.

Rayne and Julie were laughing lightly while Horatio and I continued to look from our dad to one another.

"What was that?" I asked.

"Magical night," Rayne offered as an easy explanation. "Right, Julie?"

"One expects no less in Chancellor," she answered.

"Well now," Rayne said then, turning to me. "Do you waltz, Miss Hunter? We can't let Alice and Luc think they are the only fine couple in the room."

"I do," I said, setting my hand in his. "Do you?"

"Of course."

"Well, aren't you full of surprises?"

"More than you could ever guess."

I winked at Horatio who looked decidedly uncertain, and with that, Rayne and I joined the other dancing couples, falling into step with the ballroom dance.

"Rayne! Viola!" Alice called, finally seeing us.

I smiled and waved at her.

I turned back to Rayne, who moved fluidly around the room. "Now, where did a hippie beekeeper learn how to ballroom dance?" I asked. Both Horatio and I had been forced to take lessons, and, admittedly, I'd had a lot more fun learning than Horatio did. Rayne, however, seemed a master at it.

"Oh, I pick up things here and there," he replied.

"Ah, yes, here and there. Nice place."

Rayne grinned. "Indeed. Well, I've been to a few Midsummer Night events. Very...unique. Lots of dancing. Perhaps you'll join me this year."

Midsummer. "Yeah, I was actually meaning to talk to you about that."

"About?"

"Summer."

Rayne raised an eyebrow at me. "Do tell."

"I...Luc offered me an apprenticeship in France, at his family's perfumery, for this summer. I told him I was interested."

"In France?" he said thoughtfully.

Crap. "Yeah. It's just one summer. Look, I like where we're headed, but three months is a long time to wait on someone. I'd understand if—"

Rayne pulled me closer and leaned into my ear. "Viola Hunter, I'd wait a lifetime for you."

I wrapped my arms around him. All at once my worries melted away. How foolish I'd been to believe that Rayne would even care about something like that. He was so...chill. I inhaled deeply, feeling so much happiness fill my heart that I could barely stand it.

Rayne kissed the top of my head then and said, "Besides, I know a little place in France. I haven't been there in a while. I'm due for a visit."

"In France?"

"Of course. Here and there, you know."

"Ah yes, here and there. One of these days, you should tell me a bit more about here and there, and Cassidy, and your family. The usual stuff."

"Oh, if only it were usual," he said, then added, "Of course."

I melted into him then, and we moved around the dance floor, moving in tune to the dulcet tones. The night seemed to wear away. As we glided, I saw Horatio and Julie take to the floor. Julie, it seemed, was not versed in ballroom dance, so she and Horatio invented their own style. Alice and Luc, pausing only to snatch kisses, disappeared mid-event. I saw the sparkle of Alice's blue gown as they walked outside. Before I knew it, we'd practically danced the night away.

"It's so lovely out there tonight," I said. "The cherry blossoms seem more alive under the moonlight."

"*Sakura*," Rayne said. "It's a tradition in Japan to view the cherry blossoms at night. They call it *hanami*."

"So is Japan part of here and there as well?"

Rayne laughed. "No, I just like the sushi place over by

the college. The cooks like to drink sake after hours and talk. A lot."

I laughed.

"I'll take you one night."

"Sounds great. In fact, a drink sounds perfect. Let me go get us something. Champagne?" I asked him.

"I think the gentleman is supposed to get the lady a drink," he told me.

"He is, but for the last one hour the color has been draining from Horatio's face, and he keeps patting his coat pocket. A man-to-man pep talk is in order. Midnight, right? That's when he's going to ask?" I glanced up at the clock. Unbelievably, the night had passed on the dance floor. It was almost midnight already.

Rayne nodded. "That's what he told me."

"Go tell him I said to man up. I'll send him over a whiskey and join you in a second."

Rayne nodded then headed in the direction of my brother.

Snatching a champagne off one of the trays being passed around on sliver platters, I polished off the drink as I made my way to the bar. When I arrived, I was surprised to find that I knew one of the bartenders.

"Rick?"

"Hey, Viola. I thought I saw you on the dance floor. Talked to your dad, and Horatio is everywhere tonight."

I laughed. "Yeah, it's a family affair. It's your night off. How'd you end up behind a bar?"

"Oh, my buddy, Max, works for the catering company. He was supposed to serve, but he got the flu. He called in a favor."

"Well, that sucks. Sorry your night off got ruined."

"No worries. What do you need?"

"Send my brother a whiskey?" I said with a laugh.

Rick poured the drink then instructed a server to head in Horatio's direction. Rayne patted my brother on the shoulder as the pair talked.

"And two cherry blossom champagnes," I added, but when I turned to lean against the bar, I felt an odd snap. My shoe. "Dammit," I said, then moved to sit at the chair nearest the bar. Bending, I moved to examine the heel. Sure enough, the buckle was completely off. The silver latch fell apart in my hand.

"What happened?" Rick asked, bending on his knee to examine it.

"Shoe broke," I said.

Taking my foot in his hand, Rick pulled off the heel to investigate. The nature of the move wasn't lost on me.

"Can I help?" he asked, meeting my eyes.

When he did so, I saw a certain look therein. Nope. No. Definitely not. Rick was a nice guy, but I needed to put an end to his false hopes.

I opened my mouth to tell him that I was dating Rayne now, but when I looked up, I saw Rayne cast a glance over his shoulder toward me then head out of the ballroom...and out of the building. Wait. Was he leaving? Did he think I was flirting with Rick? I looked down to see Rick was still holding my foot.

"Oh shit," I said. Pulling my foot away, I stood.

"Viola?" Rick asked.

"Look, Rick, you're a great employee and a great friend, but I think I'm pretty much falling in love with my friend who just got the wrong impression about the scene here. Got me?"

Rick nodded, stood, then handed me the shoe. "Sorry, Viola. Can't blame a guy for trying. Sorry though."

"No hard feelings."

"If you need me to explain, just let me know. It's my fault. Sorry, I feel like a douche."

"No, it's just a misunderstanding. Gotta go." I slid the broken shoe back on as best I could then ran across the ballroom after Rayne.

He was already gone by the time I got to the stairs. Alice and Luc, however, were just coming back inside. Alice, I noticed, look a bit rumpled.

"Viola? Everything okay?" Alice asked.

"I...I lost Rayne," I said, hoping in that moment that I hadn't, in fact, really lost him.

"Oh, I saw him head over to his truck," Alice said. "Almost midnight, better go in before you miss it!"

Shit! What the hell should I do now? "Okay, coming in a few."

Alice nodded and she and Luc went inside.

I walked down a few steps hoping to see Rayne's truck, but he was nowhere and my shoe had finally had enough.

"Dammit," I swore, sitting down quickly to remove my heels. Pulling both shoes off, I set them aside then rushed down the winding staircase toward the parking area...barefoot.

Before I reached the final stairwell landing, however, I saw Rayne walking back toward the building, a box in his hands.

"Rayne?" I gasped.

"What are you doing out here?" he asked, looking puzzled. "I was just brining these to you."

"Bringing...bringing what? Look, it wasn't what it looked like. Well, it kind of was. I think Rick..."

"Oh, that," Rayne said with a roll of his eyes. "Yeah, you better tell him you're off the market now."

"Wait, what?"

"Rick. You're beautiful, of course he would fall for

you. He's a good guy, though. Just let him know, and he'll be cool with it."

"Wait, you weren't upset?"

Rayne shook his head. "I trust you, Viola. Now, let's try these," he said then opened the box he was holding. Inside were a pair of amazingly beautiful silver shoes with lovely vintage-looking jewels.

"Rayne? Where did you get these?"

"A box. In my truck. Just what I needed. Curious, right?" he said with a smile.

Offering me a hand, he helped me sit. Then, moving gently, he slid the first shoe on. To my amazement, it fit like it was molded to my foot.

"Like a glass slipper," Rayne said. "That better?" He slipped on the second shoe.

I gazed down at the lovely shoes. How perfect they looked, matching my gown and glimmering in the moon-light. I closed my eyes and breathed in the cherry blossom perfumed air. "Cherry blossoms at midnight, that will be my first fragrance," I said wistfully. "Oh hell, it's midnight!"

From inside the building, I heard the clock bong out the first chime of the hour.

"Julie and Horatio!" I exclaimed, clambering to my feet.

"Let's go," Rayne said, and racing hand in hand, we

rushed back to the ballroom.

Moving through the crowd, we made our way to Julie and Horatio. Julie was chatting nonchalantly with my brother when the last chime struck the hour.

At that moment, the sky above Arden Estate crackled with fireworks, which illuminated all the stained glass in the windows of the ballroom, causing the images thereon to spring to life. And from a discreet netting suspended above Julie's table, a soft shower of cherry blossom petals began to rain down her. It was an incredibly beautiful sight.

The entire assembled audience gasped then paused to watch.

"What? What's this?" Julie asked with a laugh, holding out her hands to catch the swirling blossoms.

"Julie," my brother said then, taking her hand as he bent down on one knee. "You crashed into my world from the moment we met, changing me forever. I can't imagine spending another day without you. Julie Dayton, will you be my wife?"

I cast a quick glance around. Standing off to the side was my father who was smiling, his eyes looking watery. I noticed that Genevieve was still standing beside him. I also noticed for the first time that Julie's father was there. Alice leaned against Luc, her body melding into his. Rayne wrapped his arms around me, and we all stared as my brother produced an amazingly beautiful pink diamond ring.

Julie gazed at Horatio. It was as if she saw no one else in the room. Overhead, the sky rumbled loudly, the fireworks filling the sky with gold and pink light as the last of the cherry blossoms fell over Julie and Horatio.

"Yes," she whispered happily. "Yes!"

At that, my brother slipped the engagement ring on her finger then rose to kiss his fiancée.

The entire crowd, including all the Chancellor elite and the Japanese delegates, broke into applause. The orchestra immediately struck into Mendelssohn's *Wedding March*, which made the entire crowd laugh.

I looked up at Rayne.

"Cherry blossoms at midnight?" he said then touched my chin lightly. "Perfect."

"Perfect," I agreed, looking into Rayne's eyes.

I felt myself swoon, lost in his gaze. And when he leaned in to kiss me, there was nothing I wanted more in the world. His lips were soft and warm. I caught the heady scent of his cologne, a kind of sweet honey scent with an earthy musk undertone. The taste of his lips, sweet and salty, much like him, delighted my senses. I was lost in the honey sweetness of his kiss. My whole world was flowering open before my eyes, and it was more beautiful than anything I could have ever dreamed.

epilogue: rayne

"Ready?" I asked Alice who shifted nervously as the plane's engines rumbled to life.

"I should have had another drink," she said, checking her seatbelt for the five-hundredth time. Alice then stretched her neck, trying to look through the rows of seats in front of us at the flight attendant who was explaining aircraft safety procedures. "It's hot as Hades in here, and I can't hear what she's saying."

"Of course it's hot, it's July," I said then patted her hand. "Don't worry, you'll be safe with me."

"Even in the event the airplane falls into the sea in a fiery inferno? I've seen *Lost*, you know. If we don't drown, the smoke monster will get us."

I laughed. "You worry too much. We'll be okay. Besides, I know a mermaid who can rescue us."

"You...making with the jokes."

"Who said I was joking?" I asked her with a grin.

"Need anything else, monsieur?" an attractive red-headed flight attendant asked as she passed by.

"Maybe a drink for my friend and me?"

With a wink, she nodded.

"Hey," Alice said, "I saw that."

"I only use my twinkle for good now. My heart is off the market."

"Mine too," Alice said with a sigh. "If it wasn't, I sure as hell wouldn't be riding in this bloody tin can with wings."

I chuckled.

A few moments later, the flight attendant passed by once more. She handed me two plastic glasses and a small bottle of red wine. "*Santé*," she said then went on her way.

"Now how about that? Look," Alice said, pointing to the label: Blushing Grape Vineyards.

I laughed. "Naturally," I said then opened the bottle, pouring us both a glass. I handed one to Alice. "To love?" I lifted my glass in toast.

Alice smiled and clicked her cup against mine. "To love."

"And to happily ever after."

Continue *The Chancellor Fairy Tales* with
The Vintage Medium

Available on Amazon

about the author

New York Times and *USA Today* bestselling author Melanie Karsak is the author of *The Celtic Blood Series, The Road to Valhalla Series, The Celtic Rebels Series, Steampunk Red Riding Hood, Steampunk Fairy Tales* and many more works of fiction. The author currently lives in Florida with her husband and two children.

amazon.com/author/melaniekarsak

facebook.com/authormelaniekarsak

instagram.com/karsakmelanie

pinterest.com/melaniekarsak

youtube.com/@authormelaniekarsak

bookbub.com/authors/melanie-karsak

also by melanie karsak

The Celtic Blood Series:

Highland Raven

Highland Blood

Highland Vengeance

Highland Queen

The Celtic Rebels Series:

Queen of Oak: A Novel of Boudica

Queen of Stone: A Novel of Boudica

Queen of Ash and Iron: A Novel of Boudica

The Road to Valhalla Series:

Shield-Maiden: Under the Howling Moon

Shield-Maiden: Under the Hunter's Moon

Shield-Maiden: Under the Thunder Moon

Shield-Maiden: Under the Blood Moon

Shield-Maiden: Under the Dark Moon

The Shadows of Valhalla Series:

Shield-Maiden: Winternights Gambit

Shield-Maiden: Gambit of Blood

Shield-Maiden: Gambit of Shadows

Shield-Maiden: Gambit of Swords

THE HARVESTING SERIES:

The Harvesting

Midway

The Shadow Aspect

Witch Wood

The Torn World

STEAMPUNK FAIRY TALES:

Curiouser and Curiouser: Steampunk Alice in Wonderland

Ice and Embers: Steampunk Snow Queen

Beauty and Beastly: Steampunk Beauty and the Beast

Golden Braids and Dragon Blades: Steampunk Rapunzel

THE RED CAPE SOCIETY

Wolves and Daggers

Alphas and Airships

Peppermint and Pentacles

Bitches and Brawlers

Howls and Hallows

Lycans and Legends

THE AIRSHIP RACING CHRONICLES:

Chasing the Star Garden

Chasing the Green Fairy

Chasing Christmas Past

THE CHANCELLOR FAIRY TALES:

The Glass Mermaid

The Cupcake Witch

The Fairy Godfather

The Vintage Medium

The Book Witch

Find these books and more on Amazon!

Made in the USA
Las Vegas, NV
10 August 2023

75915534R00097